"Thorn to my Rose"

By:

C. Monet

Cover designed by Iesha Bree
Edits: by Tabitha Sharpe

C.Monet
Visit my website at www.unfilteredandundefined.com

Printed in the United States of America

First Printing: Oct. 2018

Dedication

This book is for all the wonderful women in the world that simply need to hear an I love you! You are wonderful, and you are beautifully made. Never let anyone tell you that you are too much of anything. Continue to strive and be bold!

"To Whom it may Concern,

If I never met you, I thank you for the love you've kept me from

For I have seen the spoils and anguish a lovely heart can create

I promise if ever I meet you I will run away and never look back

You've scared me straight and away from love

See when the birds chirp, I can hear your mellifluous voice

When the wind blows, I can feel your lips across my neck

When I look into the sky, I see how the heavens paint your face

With beautiful hues of blue and shades of pink

When the rain pours, I feel you cleansing me

When the sun shines, I feel your arms pulling me close and keeping me warm

When the moon glimmers and the stars smile, I feel your eyes upon me

And when the thunder booms and lightening shatters, I feel you correcting me

See if I know I love you without even meeting you, then to meet you would send me into catastrophe

For to meet you and to live all that I foresee in you, then to love you would devastate me

So to whom it may concern

If ever I meet you I thank you for the love you will destroy me with....."

Ali Strickland

Prologue

"But he that dares not grasp the thorn, should never crave the rose" Anne Bronte

10 years ago….

Ding.

Thorn: Meet me at Town Hall

Me: K

I prayed the professor didn't hear my phone going off in the middle of the lecture, as I read the text. I would never hear the end of it. But as usual Thorn needed something from me and like the puppy I was, I was on my way. Gathering my items, I excused myself and slid out of the classroom and in no time I laid eyes on my bestie pacing and talking to himself as if he was practicing for a speech. Tapping his shoulder to get his attention the look on his face scared me.

"I thought you had class." He stuttered nervously. I smiled, because I hadn't known him to stutter or lack confidence. Something was up, I could feel it.

"I did, but when Thorn needs his Rose, she appears, now what's up?" I responded hugging his waist. He smelled amazing and as usual he looked really good. His sweaters were always matched to a T, his boots always looked good on his feet and the way he wore a scarf was indescribable. I had a serious crush on someone that was born to be my best friend. The struggle was all the way real.

"Let's sit on the bench," he directed playing with his hands. I was concerned with his haste and dire need to speak with me in the middle of winter. We saw each other every day so I was worried with what he wanted that couldn't wait until we behind closed doors.

"Cool, everything ok?" I asked touching his forehead with the back of my hand. I could see the concern written on his face. I wasn't sure what feeling I would be experiencing once he finally spit out what he had to say. I was all ears, waiting to hang onto every word as usual. But the words weren't coming, just a look of discovery and a downward gaze.

7

"You know you will always be the Rose to my Thorn, right?" he asked. I laughed because this was a no brainer. We had come from once hating each other to being unable to go a few hours without speaking. What we had was real, and I doubted that anything would change that. Together or not it would be us against the world.

"Of course, what's a rose with no thorns?" I responded. I was nothing without him. I knew it, but I wondered if he knew just how much we really meant to each other. He was the pain in my ass, the light of my path, he was the rhyme to my reason. But those words would never be spoken until I felt he was ready to love me the way I loved him. Oh God, maybe that's what this about. He's finally ready to say fuck society and let's be together, I thought. I smiled widely, the sun was shining now but no sun was in sight.

"Nothing, absolutely nothing." He said.

"Damien, you are stalling just tell me. Are you transferring?" I asked cluelessly. Now my original thought of us being together was retreating and so was the warmth I once felt. I could see it in his face that this wasn't going to be a positive visit. He was face was distorted and tight. Something was wrong.

"Tru, please forgive me for what I'm about to do." Looking in my eyes made it harder for him say what he had to say. He kept looking away from me and breathing hard. Was he dying? I mean damn what was it. The suspense was killing me softly.

"Just say it Dame, I don't need you pacifying me," I said close to a scream. I could feel the tension; the heat was rising on this dreary winter day. I was starting to sweat and play out all the ways this could and would go. I felt the change in vibration when he came back from Christmas vacation.

"After graduation, I... I can't do this with you. Us can't be a thing." he spit out like it was hot lava. Now I wished I hadn't said a damn thing about him not pacifying me. I needed oxygen because that statement had just sucked all the damn air occupying my lungs.

"I don't understand. Why can't we be friends?" I asked, knowing that we had moved past friends. I understood a little, we both pretended a platonic friendship was what we had. But we were only fooling ourselves. The late-night study sessions, the hanging with each other twenty-four seven, the secret glances at each other when we kicked it. We knew, we just never addressed it. And now it was ending before it even began.

"Tru, you are too ethnic for what I have going on right now. I love it but it's not good for my image. I've decided to follow in my father's footsteps." He struggled to get out. I felt my hand twitch. I wanted to smack the shit out of him. But for some reason I didn't. This didn't sound like Thorn. This didn't sound like the man that sung the Isley Brothers to me on a daily, this wasn't the man that loved my fried chicken.

"Your mother is black, so I still don't understand what you are trying to say."

"Yea, but my mother isn't you. I've always loved that about you but now right now, it can't be that way." He confessed.

"Wow, this is bullshit and you fucking know it. I thought... I thought we had the sweetest taboo, the highest vibration, so that was all a lie?" I quizzed quickly. He was speechless he didn't have an answer and none of them would matter. His mind was made up that for some reason me, the person that was at the same school as he wasn't cut from the same cloth. Maybe I wasn't based on assets, but I had it. I had him. His back would always be covered with me. I was confused and frustrated.

We had a drunk night where sober thoughts came out and we said some shit that we couldn't take back. It wasn't a lie. I would never do anything to harm thorn or keep him from succeeding. How didn't he know that? What didn't I say and what hadn't I done. I was feeling raw and vulnerable and I didn't like it.

"That shit is and will always be true, but right now I have to focus on my future." He assured. I wasn't feeling confident because from my view it looked like I was being left behind.

"Wow, so are you saying I'm not a part of your future?" I asked finally standing to my feet.

"I have to do what's best for me and where I want to go in life. I love you Rose, I mean I really do. I want this as much as you do but we have to be honest. We need to do what's best for us both." He said.

"Why do you think you always know what's best for me? This isn't best for me this is best for you." I fussed. Our whole friendship had been based on him thinking he knew what was best for me. Which wasn't true. This... this breakup wasn't what was best for me. This would end me completely end me and from the look on his face it didn't seem that anything I could say or do would change it.

"This hurts me just as it hurts you. I'm left with no options. Please say you understand that I've got to leave this here." He begged.

"Yea, I understand. You do what you need to do, and I truly wish you luck." I said with tears in her eyes. I wasn't made I was disappointed and that was overshadowing any other emotion I was feeling. I fucked up giving him all of me when he didn't even want it. I felt my heart sinking to my feet as I cried and clutched my stomach. I was humiliated and needing to sit back down. The cry that was erupting would knock me off my feet. My heart was torn in two.

Scooting over to hug me, I moved and jumped up before he could touch me. He didn't deserve to touch me not after what he said and what he had just done. I would forever remember the look in his eyes. It was one of forgiveness and pain also. He was in nowhere near as much pain as me, that I knew for sure. This was our senior year and we had so many plans to only find out that none of that would be happening, well not together, not as a team. The disrespect I felt again made my hand twitch. I pinched myself, maybe I was dreaming.

"I'm sorry," he muttered. I'm sure he meant it, but it didn't eliminate the anguish I felt currently. That apology was a temporary band aid that would only fall off and expose the same pain all over again. The position we were in was uncomfortable and completely ignorant. It almost made no sense, I came from a good home, we were in the same college, and we were both driven and we both had dreams. But without saying it, I was too black for him. I was too flawed to be on his arm as he climbed his way to the top.

"Yea me too, I'm sorry that my black intimidates you, I'm sorry that you for whatever reason think that I can't contribute to your success, and I'm really sorry that you will never know a love like mine. I love you, Thorn. Always have. Even when I knew it would never be more than what it was. And now all you have to say is sorry for breaking my heart and ultimately telling me that I'm too black. You sound just like them and I feel bad for you. I wish you luck and success." Caressing his face, I left him sitting right there on that bench with my heart in his pocket.

I felt him watching me leave but as the coward he was he didn't chase after me, which only added to the agony. He knew there was no coming back from the racist shit he had just spewed. I couldn't believe him. I couldn't wrap my head around how he was even able to form those hurtful sentences. Why did I put him on pedestal? Why didn't I know better? Fuck him, I wasn't going to repair this open wound with lots of alcohol to numb the pain and reflection on discernment or the lack thereof. I mean damn this whole time I had been out here emotionally unprotected. I had been in the company of someone that hadn't had my best interest at heart. He was a piece of shit for this.

I would be great, I would be something, I would be everything they didn't want me to be. Angelus Silesius said that 'The Rose is without explanation she blooms because she blooms'. I was about to bloom and never look back at the greatness they tried to stifle.

Raven's Pointe

"Ma, I'm really sorry about cancelling dinner. I promise to make it up to you," I mumbled, speaking with my mother over the car phone. I hated cancelling plans with her, especially for a damn meeting I had no desire to attend in the first damn place. *"I'll do anything to make it up to you. Just tell me what it is."*

I'm Trulicity Rose McCall, a private investigator and true rose from the concrete. I was hard on the outside but soft as a teddy bear when it mattered the most. Listening to my mother sigh depressed me. Meetings currently ran my life, whether it be for work or it be for SSRP, the Secret Society of Ravens Pointe, bullshit. It was a pain in the ass, but once in, there was rarely a way out. Our group and my second job was much like a gang but without the painful jumping in scenario. Some loved it, and there were a few like me that hated it. I was the only woman, the only black woman at that, and well, I was a smart ass that didn't mind telling anyone like it was. That made the boys uncomfortable and uneasy, so now I'm speeding, running the risk of getting a ticket, to see the smug faces I hated so much.

"You work too much, baby, take a break if you want to make it up to me." I heard my mother's voice say over the speakers. She was right. It was a catch twenty-two. I loved what I did, but in the same breath could say I detested it. I mean, uncovering the truth for people was an amazing thing, it was the rose; while tearing families apart was the thorn. I assumed every job had moments like that, and that's what kept me pushing.

'Tru Findings LLC' was all mine and located in the heart of the city. My office was surrounded by sky rises, parking garages, and the best eateries the town had to offer. I thought I would be proud when I graduated college, but my proudest moment came when I secured this building and put my degree to use. I've seen enough bullshit between work and SSRP, to leave relationships, friendships, and mergers on the back burner. I spent my days working cases that didn't make the news, and at night, I spent my time capturing all the ugly moments no one wanted you to see. I was undeniably the best at what I did. I was discreet, efficient, and deadly with my skill set.

If you didn't want to get caught, you shouldn't do the dirt, that was the motto at my firm. It was my life. I worked so hard for everything they didn't want me to have, and no one was going to take it away from me. It was imperative that I did what I had to do in order to take my firm global, but these things I had to do didn't always make me happy, such as cancelling on my Friday night chill session with my mother, and I hoped she knew that.

"I know, Momma; I know." I agreed as I gripped the steering wheel harder. I was frustrated with all the shit I had on my plate. I couldn't let her know that, so I kept my responses short. She wasn't aware of all the things I had on my calendar, and that's how I wanted to keep it. It was difficult, but I had to press on. Dealing with other's shit helped me ignore my own shit, and plus, I had to do my due diligence to the public. Until ignorant people stopped being ignorant, until the cheaters stopped cheating, and until the greedy stopped being greedy, and until I was ready to unpack my baggage, I had a job to do. I prayed she'd understand and cut me some slack. *"Do you need dinner, ma?"* I felt so shitty cancelling, knowing how much she looked forward to our weekly dinner plans.

"Tru, don't you worry about me. Go handle business. You know I ain't above eatin' left overs." She chuckled. My mother's understanding tone was always soothing. *"Just call me when you get home."* She was always so willing to put me first, even as a child, but I desired to do better for her. She was getting older, and my dad was never home. He was a train conductor, and his hours were ridiculous. She needed me, and I needed her.

"I love you, Momma. Don't wait up for me."

"Tru, you need to be careful running those streets all time of night." She fussed. I knew I wasn't going to get off that easy.

"I will, Momma." I promised, disconnected the call just in time for me to start heading into my meeting. I thought about what she said. I tried really hard to be careful but as the days went on it became more difficult. I took risks, that was my drug; it was my habit, but when the adrenaline of those risks wore off, and the voices in my head started, I was reminded of how reckless I was.

"See you later," I whispered.

I lived on my own but certain times I felt safer sleeping in my old room. So, that's what I did. Damn, that sounded good right about now. I'd could relax with my momma while enjoying some good wine, a cheese plate, and *Dirty Dancing* for the millionth time. I doubted it would happen tonight. She wasn't a night owl like me.

"Let's get this shit over with," I said, checking my wild hair in the mirror.

Arriving at the restaurant, I wondered what the hell they could possibly need from me this time. If it wasn't one thing, it was another. *"Hey Tru, I need you to sacrifice a fucking leg today!"* I joked and laughed as I pulled into my destination. Shit was also off the wall for me. It was never something morally acceptable or light. Everything they asked of me was heavy and morally inept. It was the shit they were too coward to complete themselves that they often tasked me with as if I didn't have morals and a personal code to live by.

Pulling up to the front door of The Rave, I valeted my fancier than needed car and strolled inside. I was in a somewhat happy mood, not sure why. The day had been long from the few cases I had to complete,

15

but none the less, I was feeling good about Friday. I personally loved Friday's. It signified the end of the week, the rest and relaxation coming from the weekend.

Raven's Pointe was a big town inside of the state of Avia. It held big mentality, pretentious boys claiming to be men, and spoiled brats that felt oppression was a choice, much like Kanye. I loved the town although I couldn't stomach the people. As a PI, I knew something about everyone, but the rolling hills, blue skies, and perfectly green grass, made it close to impossible to leave. We rarely had cloudy days. Mostly dry, always sunny, and always perfect.

"Emilio, looking good!" I greeted as I made my way to the back of the pub. Reaching the off sides door, I knocked four times and kicked the corner. Within seconds, I watched the door slide back, granting entrance into the secret society's lair. As usual, I broke into a fit of coughs from the cigar smoke. I could barely see my enemies from all the smoke filling the room.

"Damn, Ryan. You knew I was coming, and you couldn't wait to light that funky ass cigar?" I asked fanning the smoke from my face. It was a rhetorical question, but I had to ask. He never failed to piss me off on purpose. It was either his scratchy, nasally voice, his cigar smoke, or the fact that he thought he owned me, or that I somehow owed him something more than my offered services.

"Tru, you know after a day at the office, a good cigar is my favorite." Ryan was a nuisance, a pain in the ass, and the reason I was a part of this detestable secret society. Ryan and I should be best buds. We've only known each other since freshman year in college, but what was once a promising friendship, turned into utter confusion amongst us. His lies and my attitude just didn't mix. We fought and battled like an old couple after thirty years of marriage.

"Yes, I know, but after a long day of work, I'd like to survive until I can enjoy my favorite things." I knew he would be offended. I'd made it clear several times that I had no desire to be a part of such a pompous cause as this. It served no real purpose in my life or the town's. It was simply compiled of a bunch of rich white men wanting to play God and rule the universe. I despised it. Yet, here I was, waiting to find out why I had been summoned this time.

"I'm offended, Tru! You don't think I care about your favorite things?"

"You know you don't. Now, why am I here?" I asked, tired of dancing Ryan's dance. He wanted me here for a reason, and I needed to know why and fast. It was close to nine p.m., and it was almost time for me to make my moves and find out what Mr. Lebler had been up to since I had already cancelled plans with my momma. Ryan was wasting my time like always.

"Ok, ok, I have a job for you. It requires your expertise, you know, that spying thing you love so much."

Rolling my eyes, I remembered why me and Ryan weren't friends anymore. He was a minimizer, always attempting to make someone feel small and unimportant. With that thought, I asked, "Why can't your sister do it?"

Ryan's sister, Colleen, was my best friend. We understood each other, and we worked the same job, so why I was the pick for this 'spying thing' boggled my mind. She was capable of doing his dirty work just as much as I was.

"Damien," Ryan replied with a swivel of his chair/ "You look stunning, Tru. That afro gets larger every time I see you. Magnificent," he said, clearly taken back. I wanted to throw up on the expensive

Persian rug that adorned the floor. I wasn't desperate enough to appreciate his compliments.

"Bring it back, Ryan. Who, what, when, and where?" I snapped my fingers, bringing his attention back to the matter at hand. I would never get in bed with Ryan, and he knew it, and he needed to never forget it. I had too much respect for myself, and I also cared way too much about his sister to lie with sleeping dogs.

"He's running for senator, and we need all the dirt you can find on him. You have a month." I studied Ryan, and something was off about his request. No eye contact, just a sly grin on his old, scarred face. He was lying. I knew the lying face all too well from Ryan. We had history, and I think he forgot that sometimes. Speaking of history, I thought back to the day we all first met.

The sun was shining so bright, I knew I'd be partially blind if I didn't find refuge. I needed refuge from a lot actually. It was my first day of college, and my parents were hanging on to me like flies on shit. I was ready to start my new life as an independent adult. I just received a full ride to one of the best schools Avia had to offer. The spectacular criminal justice program was why I was here. I worked hard to get here, and my parents were stopping me from living my best life.

"Now Rose, remember what I taught you. Left hook, right hook, jab." My father enacted. I smiled because I knew they were on the onset of empty nest syndrome. They would miss me as I would them, but it was my independence that scared them so much. I had never been a wild child, but the idea of me leaving home and being hours away rustled something in them and me.

"Daddy, I'll be fine. You taught me well." I promised, giving them the last hug until I got a break and could come home. "Mama, I got all my snacks, and I got the blankets. Try not to worry." I wasn't worried about my dad, just my mother; she would be so alone now with him being gone also. I had already suggested she get a cat or something, but she refused, promising she would make herself busy at church.

"Oh, baby, please come see me first chance you get," she said with tears in her eyes hugging me tighter.

"I promise, Momma." I kissed her and waved bye and headed to my dorm to try and get settled in.

"Ahh." I grunted as the heavy wood door went into my gut. I was so focused on the breakdown my mom was having that I completely forgot I was in front of the door. The pain would ensure I never lost track of my movements. First lesson of college--pay attention.

"I'm so sorry, I didn't see you," he said helping me pick up my books. It was odd, only because he was white. We had come a long way, but not this far. I made up one percent of the black people that attended this school, and to hear an apology for an accident was unusual.

"Thank you, it's my fault. I wasn't paying attention." I smiled as he handed me my books back. "Rose," I said extending my hand.

"Ryan Scott," he answered with a small smile. He was a little off, not in a 'I rape college girls' way but in a 'aha, a girl finally noticed me' way. He looked like the type of guy that was all about his studies and a loner. He smiled a pearly white smile, with his perfect blonde hair and blue eyes. It was cute, he was cute, but I was only being polite.

"Nice to meet you, Ryan, and thanks again," I said gathering all my things back up, preparing to enter my dorm and ultimately start a new life. He lingered, and I turned around to see what he was ogling at.

"Nice fro, it's pretty sweet," he complimented with another smile.

I smiled and continued to my dorm. My fro was my life, my signature. It was my Foxy Brown look, and it fit my figure and my face. Eventually, I would be on some Diana Ross type shit, so to receive a compliment on it from a slick-haired white man made me happy. Maybe it won't be so bad here after all. I came to college, well, this college, with the impression of being stoned for my skin color.

"Tru, earth to Tru." Ryan snapped, bringing me back to the present day, back to the pain of what our friendship became once we all grew up and the world got its claws in us. Ryan became the devil disguised with blue eyes, and I became the token black girl with an off the chart attitude and slim patience for bullshit.

"Yeah my bad, what were you saying?" I asked. Not wanting to bring it to his attention at the moment, I grabbed the manila folder off of the mahogany table and got the shock of my life. It was my first love; well, he didn't know that. No, yes he did; he just didn't act on it. "Damien?" I asked. The name didn't ring a bell at first because it had been years since he was in town or sitting on the frontal lobe of my brain, he was always the traveler. Last I heard was that he was in Alias, the next city over. Not to mention once you hurt me, I placed you in the deepest pit of my brain. I wasn't letting anyone come back from the grave and put me in it instead. I had to tell Ryan no and mean it.☐

The Answer is NO

"I can't do it." I advised. It was too close--way too close, I'd stumble and ultimately fuck this up. It was a NO for me. Damien and I ended terribly, and truthfully, that chapter was never officially or properly closed. This job could fuck with my money and be a waste of time. Damien had always been fucking perfect. He never missed a beat. I'd be grasping for straws trying to find dirt on him and his party.

"You don't have a choice; it has to be handled. We cannot let this... this -"

"This *black* man?" I questioned with a raised eyebrow. I always allowed Ryan to pretend that he wasn't a racist prick, but he truly was. He was the worst kind; the one that pretends to like black people. You know, they have that one black friend. The one that's fucked a few black girls, and now they're woke and lovers of my people. That was Ryan. I liked my racists, racist, not straddling the fence.

"His color is not an issue. I have black friends. Remember Khalil? And what about you?" He quizzed. See what I meant? Khalil of all people. I shook my head because this wasn't the Ryan I knew.

"We aren't friends, just colleagues. Don't get that shit confused." I corrected.

"Either way, we need your expertise. Only you can complete a task like this. Plus, I know you two have history. He will trust you and open up," he responded.

"He also knows Colleen. Ryan, I don't want to be involved with this shit. Damien and I ended badly, and you know that," I said sternly. I needed to stand my ground, or this organization would continue to run over me and run my damn life. For years, I'd allowed them to give me the grit and grimy jobs with no regard for my own personal feelings, and it stopped today.

"Run along, Tru, we are on limited time," he said dismissing me. He couldn't even look me in my face because he knew this was some straight malarkey. He was a coward. He knew this was a dummy mission after all the things me and Damien went through and the way he carried himself.

"Such a bitch." I laughed snatching his cigar from his mouth and dropping it in his drink. Grabbing the folder, I repeated the knock and strolled out the door. I was furious, I didn't want to be a part of this at all.

Storming out the bar, I watched the patrons stumble and request more alcohol. I never understood why people didn't drink in the privacy of their own homes. It was silly to be out in public making a fool of yourself. I learned the most about people while pretending to be drunk while they were really drunk. People loved to feel like they had someone just like them.

Laughing as I walked to my car, it was just like fate to put Damien back in my damn life when I specifically asked for him not to be. I mean, I made sure he wasn't. I changed my number, requested a transfer from the dorms, and I blocked him from my mind. *I don't want this,* I said to myself walking to my car.

The air was brisk but heavenly. It was the perfect weather for a walk down the avenue, but I was exasperated, so walking wouldn't be in the cards. I needed a drink and some alone time.

My head was banging at the realization that my talents would be used to bring down another black man, a black man that wanted to make changes; a black man that used to be the thorn to my rose. I smiled thinking about that silly saying he used to say to me, but it instantly went sour from the realization of how things played out after they seemed so promising.

Why me? I couldn't understand why it had to be me. Yes, we had history. We grew up together, but that didn't mean we had that history now. It had been years since Damien Thorn cast me to the side for a more fitting spouse. I shouldn't care. Our senior year, he all but told me I was too black to come along for the ride to being the Raven Pointe President. *Fuck him,* I thought.

Too Much of Anything

If you enjoy the fragrance of a rose, you must accept the thorns which it bears-

Isaac Hayes

For years, I struggled with being "too" much of anything. I covered up my dark skin, I permed my hair, and I used my inside voice or didn't speak at all. He deserved to be brought down for that bullshit alone. He didn't really care about the black people in Raven Pointe; he cared about success. It had always been that way, but I struggled with the idea of playing the "you hurt me, I hurt you" game. I knew hearts didn't break even, and I couldn't handle the idea of being heartbroken again by Damien Malik Thorn.

Pulling into the park on Damascus, I pulled his file out and studied it. I had to see what he had been up to. I hoped it would be the determining factor of whether or not I'd actually do the job, but as I glanced over his accolades, he had been up to exactly what I thought he had been up to: succeeding, gaining the world, and looking scrumptious doing it. The smile that appeared on my face, scared me. He still had a hold on me.

"I can't do this. I need to call Colleen," I said to myself. She would be the voice of reason and the one person that was of sound mind.

Ringing her phone, she answered in no time. She was reliable like that. It didn't matter what time I called or what I needed, she would be there waiting and ready to assist. Colleen and I met by way of her older brother, Ryan. Both in criminal justice classes, we hit it off, but Colleen was different; she wasn't like Ryan. She loved life and let others live theirs no matter their color, upbringing, or financial status. My girl was beautiful, smart, and talented just like me. I always joked that we hit it off because she was just as nosey as I was.

"Hey, girl." She cooed.

24

"Colleen, I can't take this job Ryan gave me. It's bullshit."

"I hate my own brother for always fucking with you. Aren't I horrible?"

"I mean, not really. He's a toupee wearing shit bag. What's to love?" We laughed as I waded in the water before telling her the task that was put before me. I already knew what she would say. She knew all about me and Damien and how the shit played out ten years ago. She despised him too. She went as far as approaching and telling him exactly how stupid he was. She told him that she hoped someone broke his heart and left him with only a box of Saltine crackers in the cabinet. The day she came back to our dorm and told me, I laughed until I cried.

"What's the job, and how can I help?" she asked.

"It's Damien. He wants to me to ruin his life, so he can't become the senator. I feel horrible even thinking of doing it, but what other choice do I have?" I couldn't go against the rules of the society, not unless I wanted to lose my practice and my clout within Avia. SSRP did one positive thing; it took care of its members. If you had something you needed done, they got it handled. The available resources of SSRP was one of the few roses in the bed of thorns.

"Damien? Damien?" She quizzed.

"Yes, my first love and hell, only love." I realized what a travesty that was after saying it out loud. It was true. After my split or whatever you called me and him, I threw myself into work and made sure my dreams manifested. I wanted to prove him wrong and somehow show him that I wasn't who he thought I was. I couldn't wait to be successful, prim and effective.

"Why can't you do it after how that asshole treated you?"

I knew she would say that. She was my comrade, and she didn't want to see me hurt, but truthfully, I always held hope that he would come back, understanding and regretting the mistake he made, "Tru, you are a rose; you are beautiful. He didn't deserve you then, and he doesn't deserve you now," she said softly. She could hear my thoughts.

"I know, but we have history. Isn't it a little childish to fight back with fire?"

"I suppose, but he started the shit! Fuck that guy," she answered. She was correct, but I had nothing to gain from ruining his life. Running Raven Pointe had always been his dream. Being in power had always been his dream, and truthfully, we needed a new face in this town.

"Hearts don't break even," I responded.

"I know this, but at least you can get your fucking peace back."

"Yeahh, but what about his goals to make us an equal people?" I asked.

"If you don't do it, someone else will. I know it sucks to be you, but listen, someone will do it, or they will assassinate him."

I love the place, but nothing about this town was made for the likes of 'us'. I had to wear my hair natural because there was no possible way the town beautician would know what to do with my hair. My clothes were close to gothic unless I wanted to be in silk suits and heels all day. For my skin, I had to go to the next town over to get any skin care products. Ryan and his buddies didn't want that to change, and by the looks of Damien's profile, that's exactly what he was set out to do. His campaign was centered around supporting black businesses, giving us positions of power and making it a level playing field for the less fortunate. What type of person would I be if I stopped that? I was them, and they were me. Had it not been for the society, my success wouldn't have come so easily. We needed him.

"I know that much, but he wants to make some changes, and I stand behind them. This is a conflict of interest, and your brother fucking knows it."

"I can talk to him and see what he says. If he doesn't agree, I'll take over the Lebler case." She groaned.

"You would do that for me?" I asked already knowing the answer. She would do anything for me, as I would for her. I was thankful to have someone so supportive. I didn't deserve her, and I knew that, but if she did this for me, I would owe her big time.

"Yes, I'll let you know what he says."

"I love you, vanilla bean," I said, disconnecting. I decided to make a visit to Damien's loft just to get an idea of what I might be dealing with. He probably lived in some sky rise that over looked the city. It was probably heavily guarded and impossible to penetrate. He probably slept on silk sheets in a gay ass canopy bed. He always thought he was royalty, some fucking king, but to me, he was just Damien Thorn, and if I took this job, I would have to treat him as such. Nothing would be off limits or too inappropriate to share.

The Thorn

The sweat dripping down my forehead scared me. I was hot to touch but freezing internally. What the fuck happened? I couldn't see shit with this bright ass light in my face. It was blinding me.

"Hello" I called out in the sterile white room. I didn't remember getting here, and I didn't know how long I had been in this room going through death. I could hear conversation, but no one was answering me. I was freezing so bad my teeth were chattering, but the sweat, it was so much sweat. Maybe I had the flu, but I didn't remember being sick. Nothing was adding up, and that was frustrating me.

"Hello, can someone help me?" I attempted to move my arms, but the restraints kept me from moving. They were so tight, leather. Was I in a mental ward? I mean, I had done some crazy shit but nothing that a crazy house would solve.

Click!

I closed my eyes at the loud sound of the pen clicking. Why the hell was that so loud? I still couldn't see anyone or make out where I was. I tried to recall any actions or events that led me here, but I was coming up short. A lone tear escaped my eye. Fear was setting in, and the veins in my body were crawling and protruding like vines growing up a tree.

"HELP" I screamed at the top of my lungs gripping the strap that had my arm. My body felt weak, unstable and not like my own. I didn't have control, and as my heart started to beat faster and faster, his face came into view.

"Welcome back," he whispered.

Honk

Honk.

"Move out the way, crazy!" a man from behind me yelled out his car window.

Throwing my hand up, I apologized for holding up the light. I must have fallen asleep at the red light. I needed to get it together and soon. Sleep deprivation was a bitch, and mine was catching up to me. I should've been turning around to call it a night, but in true nature, I pressed on. Sleep was for the weak.

On Second Thought

Boloro was the next town over and mostly comprised of farm land and larger than life homes. This town was designed for the politicians and the major decision makers. If you were important, you lived here. I doubted that the people that lived here even wanted to. There was literally nothing there. There were no jazz clubs, no shopping malls, and no real humans, unlike Raven's Pointe. I still proceeded. Crossing the old bridge, I could already see the difference. The streets weren't littered with lights, and the roads were empty. This case now had my interest. I mostly wanted to see Damien in the flesh. I'm sure his photos did him no justice.

When we met at nineteen, he was already fine: chocolate brother, very clean cut, skinny. His freshman fifteen hadn't reached him yet, and his teeth were perfect like chiclets. His parents were wealthy, so he wore suits even as a child. His taste in fashion had only gotten better as an adult. I could bet he was rocking no less than a two-thousand-dollar suit daily. His prude ass was probably wearing them to bed. His waves were always top notch, his cologne and hygiene were that of a metrosexual. He didn't do funk, and he didn't half step when he stepped out the door.

"All you had to do was just keep it real," I said to myself thinking of what we could have been. If it sounded like I was trying to convince myself that what I was doing was acceptable, you are right. *"I could have loved you and uplifted you."* My voice was somber, and that enraged me. I was doing just fine until this fucking job and the mere mention of his name. He hadn't crossed my mind in years. It didn't matter how many times my mom brought him or his family up, I left it there like trash on the curb. Gone. No longer an issue for me.

Damien Thorn was a sellout, well, that's what we called successful black men that wanted to be something other than the norm. There was nothing wrong with him wanting to be a senator or president; it was the path he intended to take to get there that irked me. Technically, he was still a sellout. He earned that term when he crushed my soul about being too black. Can you believe that shit? He all but told me that my blackness would be a bad look for him. "Tuh." I breathed.

I remembered going home for summer break and changing everything about who I was. I stopped going by Rose, that name didn't suit me anymore. She was too innocent and dumb. I made an honest effort to move forward, but I slipped into a depression. I cried so much I was positive a river dwelled within me. The tears fell like the rain. It was months after my heartbreak that I realized just how cleansing the tears were for my soul. I shed the skin of the old me and took a new form.

Damien left me so embarrassed and humiliated. He probably didn't even know why I left school for a little while after that. He was so full of himself and selfish. He had no idea that I was all about him and really just waiting for him to say he wanted me the same. How many times did we have to have an awkward moment for him to realize that my feelings were present? How many times did I have to hint at being more than study buddies? He never took me seriously because he had his eyes set on a white woman that would raise his kids while he went state to state grinning that shit eating grin I adored.

There was no doubt in my mind that we could have been great. We could have been better than great. He just didn't want to look deep enough within me to see my worth. It was all about the surface. I didn't matter if I was timid and quiet, my skin would have always been the issue, and he knew it.

Shaking my head, I pulled up slowly and hit the car lights. Grabbing my bag and camera, I stepped out and covered my head. This was the norm for me, concealed and stealthy. His condo was well lit, and the cute little beetle in the driveway, let me know he had a female companion. I grinned. "Figures," I muttered, snapping a picture of the vehicle. This was going to be easy, if and when I decided to take the bait thrown at me.

Scanning the area, I found my spot. The things I was able to see would have been missed by the naked eye. I truly had a knack for what I did. It came easy to me. It was due to my strong observant quality, but it was mostly due to me being a 'super'.

That's what I was thinking about before the car started honking. How it all happened was nuts and sometimes scary when I think about what I put myself through during that dark time. After shit hit the fan with Damien, I had a wild night with Ryan, the scientist. Ryan had a knack for the sciences when he wasn't being a total asshole, and somehow, he was able to convince my dumb ass to be his test monkey. I agreed hoping it would give me leverage. It was such a stupid decision when I thought about it. Staring at Damien through his living room window reminded me just how stupid I was.

"Rose, wake up." I heard as the once again bright light was in my face blinding me. My arms were free, and my body wasn't full of sweat. I groaned as I adjusted to move myself up on the hospital bed.

"What happened?" I asked looking at my arms and body and around the room. It wasn't familiar, but the person in front of me was. That gave me some relief, not a lot because my body felt strange. It was sensitive to touch.

"We did it." He beamed. I covered my ears, they were so sensitive. "Rose, we did it."

"Did what?" I asked tense from his high pitch voice. "Ryan, did what?" I asked again. I hoped we didn't have sex. I would never be able to live with myself if I slept with him. I would take it to the grave and kill him, so it never came out.

"You don't remember?" he asked confused. I rolled my eyes at his line of questions. I asked because I didn't know what happened, why repeat what I said? It wouldn't change my lapse of memory.

32

"No Ryan, I don't remember. Where the hell am I, and what have you done to me?" I felt funny as hell and groggy. The light was too much, sound was too much. All my senses were heightened, and I didn't like it one bit.

"The experiment was a success." He smiled proudly.

"Oh shit," I said as my stomach instantly felt queasy. The realization of what I allowed him to do to me hit me like a ton of bricks. I couldn't process that I said yes to him injecting me with a turkey baster, and now he was saying that it went fine. Was I a mutant? Do I have extra legs or multiple arms? Is my eye cocked? He must have sensed the look and nature of my thoughts.

"Let me help you out the bed," he said jumping to his feet. Moving slowly out of fear not pain, I slowly walked to the mirror in the bathroom, and I looked normal. I mean, my eyes had bags under them and my hair needed a hot comb bad, but all my limbs were in place, my face looked the same. Nothing to the eye looked different. I breathed a sigh of relief.

"So, what changed?" I asked, still rubbing my face in the mirror. Once I thought I had it figured out, more questions arose. Running my hands through my hair out of confusion, I prayed my mother never found out what I did because she would kill me and schedule an exorcism. My mother didn't believe in Satan's work.

Moving my hands in front of my face, I tried to see what my powers were. I vaguely remembered why I even agreed to this. I wanted to be better than Thorn thought I was, and I wanted to get my mind off of his flighty ass. It was no luck because I still felt my heart broken in a million pieces. I was still wondering what Thorn was up to and if he was thinking of me.

"Ahh, it's me, Rose!" Ryan screamed.

Growling, it took me a minute to realize who it was that I had jacked up and pinned on the wall. My skin was glowing soft hues of red, my veins were bulging, and I felt nothing. I effortlessly had Ryan off the ground looking petrified.

"I'm sorry, Ryan." I didn't know what that was, but I felt something that wasn't there. It happened so quickly; one minute I was wondering if Thorn was thinking of me, and the next, I had rage in my heart and strength to raise Ryan from the ground.

"It worked, it fucking worked." he laughed with tears in his eyes. This was a happy moment for him, and pieces of me were just as happy to be a part of it with him, but my nerves and the concerns were outweighing that. I knew nothing about being a superhero or having any powers. I barely wanted to do the work required of me now.

"That's great, now what?" I asked.

That night changed my life for better and worse. The experiment he involved me in gifted me with abilities to defy gravity, see through walls, and supersonic hearing. After that night, shit got a little scary for me, but I managed to use it to my good once I gained control.

I enjoyed using my abilities to help others and gain my paycheck, but like everything else, there were always thorns that come with the roses. Because Ryan felt as though he made me who I am, he felt that he owned me. Which in fact I was the one that added value to his portfolio, not the other way around. Thinking about it, I realized I wasn't much different from Damien. I was willing to lay down with the devil to have my own idea of success. Now I was left with no sleep, always having to overthink, and be alert. I thought it would bring me some level of freedom from the toxic feeling I had about myself, but in return, it only turned me into a toxic person if I didn't control myself.

"Fuck Ryan also," I mumbled. Ryan's cruelty knew no bounds. He normally conducted his study on animals but when he presented what we believed to be groundbreaking research, I couldn't say no. I needed to feel some sort of power in my moment of weakness.

I was the first human he ever tested the concoction on. He turned me into a bad ass. It was a proud moment when I jumped six stories.

Now, I use it to sniff out who's man was cheating in the sky rises and who was skimming off the top at work. It wasn't noble work all the time, but I enjoyed bringing those that were deserving, the truth. But as I peered into Damien's window, I wondered who I would be bringing truth to by exposing any secrets he had. Knowing Damien, he probably had no secrets. He was a square, always playing by the rules, always saying exactly what you wanted to hear even if it was a lie.

"Dame, please tell me you aren't eating that horrible food?" little miss perfect asked. I could feel the agitation coursing through my veins at her voice. Her stringy blonde hair was in a perfect bun, she even had shoes on still and her skirt was at the perfect length. This is what he wanted? Someone that stayed in the lines just like him. "Lame," I whispered while in the bushes.

"Erica, I love fried chicken and it's my cheat day." He grinned.

I almost passed out from watching him grin. His teeth were still perfect and the contrast against his brown skin made me cream in my panties. This was why I wouldn't be able to get anything accomplished on this job. He was still fine, drop dead gorgeous almost. He had gained weight, good weight. He was beefy, healthy and filling out his dress shirt quite nicely.

"I don't know how you eat that disgusting, greasy food." Erica rolled her eyes.

I wanted to slap some sense into them both. He didn't owe her an explanation on his eating habits. He was a grown man and black. He loved fried chicken like we all did. What the hell was she talking about disgusting? She could serve to eat a real meal or two. If I had the opportunity, I would tell little miss Erica how much he loved watermelon and grape soda also. All that stereotypical shit he loved and all the things she probably turned her plastic surgery nose up to.

"I don't complain about you eating hummus day in and day out."
He laughed. I can't believe he laughed and so did she. She was dying of
laughter, red in the face, tears in her eyes. I personally didn't find a
fucking thing funny about the situation or the conversation. This was
the bullshit I be talking about. I guess you could say I was in my
feelings and felt slightly jaded at his corny ass. He robbed me of the
opportunity to laugh at his corny jokes, it wasn't fair.

Was my fried chicken eating ass unworthy of the likes of Damien?
Snapping a few pictures, I decided to call it a night. Nothing exciting
was happening here. Erica was a pole that I wouldn't even enjoy
watching get off and Damien, well, he would have his day. Mission
Accepted.

Damien's Thorns

"When we get married, you will love hummus just as much as I do." Erica smiled. I didn't. The talk of marriage was starting to drive me up a wall. I wasn't ready for marriage. At least not with Erica or her perfect family. She was perfect for my image and that was about it. My mans operated when I was with her, but it wasn't that star-studded dick that a woman deserved from someone she loved.

The people pleaser in me knew that we couldn't disappoint. *The oldest children from two of the most prominent families in Avia tying the knot*' That's what the headlines would read. Nothing about it would capture love and happiness. I didn't want do it, even though my mother had been down my throat about the circumstances of our relationship. She could sense the distance or lack of love but, yet she still insisted on this nuptial taking place. The thought of it made my palms sweat. The idea of reciting untruthful vows disgusted me and made me see marriage as nothing but a piece of paper. It was deplorable.

I was on the brink of success. I could taste it, but my heart wasn't in it anymore. I didn't want it if it meant had to comply and marry for status. That wasn't me. I don't understand how marriage became about status and not compatibility. I used to think my parents, Dewayne and Darlene, had something real. It was when they started going to their lawyers to negotiate their contracts, my heart was crushed. It was all a lie and I knew then that this is what they expected from me.

"I doubt it. You stayin' tonight?" I asked, hoping like hell she said no. I was fed-up with laying with a stick figure every night. Her hair in my brushes annoyed me, her thin lips depressed me, and her obnoxious laugh made my ears hurt. I don't know how I planned to do this for years to come. According to my mother, I would be on the road so much I wouldn't see much of her and as long as I kept my affairs out of the public eye I could live a normal life. There was nothing normal about that.

"Damien." She smiled. Erica Wainwright was a beautiful woman and would make someone extremely happy one day, just not me. I wanted a woman with a voice, one that would stand up for herself and for me. I didn't want someone pat me on the back and secretly suggest I do as I was told. But with the road I was on, I couldn't have that. I couldn't have a woman that complimented me or gave me strength in my moments of weakness. My spouse had to be young, dumb, and possibly blonde.

"What I do?" I smiled back.

"You know I can't stay tonight. Father said that as close as we are to winning the election we can't afford any scandals. Chat with you tomorrow?" she suggested.

"Yeah sure, maybe we can do lunch or something." I wanted to shout hell yeah and Crip walk in my kitchen. I was sick of looking at her, and she had only been over for an hour. That hour was enough to solidify my reasoning for not bothering with her. She didn't like fried chicken, that was a no go.

"Perfect, get with my assistant" she replied, kissing me on the lips and grabbing her jacket and purse. We couldn't even date naturally, everything went through our assistants. What type of shit was that?

"Sure thing" I advised closing the door and watching her from my window to her car. My momma would ring my neck if she knew I wasn't being a gentleman and walking Erica to her car. She was a black belt in Tae Kwando; she didn't need me. Plus, I hoped some masked men jumped out and took her ass down to the river bank. That was fucked up, but I damn sure didn't care. Here lately my thoughts hadn't even been my own. It felt good to have a funny thought and let it linger.

Turning from the window, I noticed an unknown vehicle parked up the road. It was out of place for sure, no one else lived over here. The

Bolo' was a new condominium that I owned. I was surprised to see a vehicle, but I wasn't surprised that someone was watching. I was three months away from becoming the next senator and then after that, I would be claiming the presidency, God willing. I knew eventually the reporters, PI's and papers would be sending their best investigators out to spy and ultimately ruin my chances. I was better than this and that's what they failed to realize. Had they caught me back in college they would have a leg to stand on. Now I colored inside the lines, I did what I was told, and I kept myself out of shit. Life was boring.

Flipping a bird at the car, I turned back to focus on chilling for just a moment alone. A part of me hoped that someone found something on me. I was tired of pretending to be someone I wasn't. I listened to classical music but played old school Tupac when I was alone. I liked wearing basketball shorts and slides instead of suits and tight ass shoes. I liked watching a little crap T.V instead of watching the debate. I wanted to go back to being a simple man. But it was impossible when you born to be a senator and born to make your parents proud.

For now, I would close the doors and my windows and be Thorn, my alter ego. I turned on *Ambitionz Az a Rider* by Tupac, got comfortable. I took my Popeye's to my room ate on my now messy bed and relaxed. I deserved it every now and again. I had been on the road for months shaking hands and kissing ugly ass babies. My jaws hurt from smiling so much. Now, it was time to wait for the election, keep my nose clean and hope I'd come out on top.

"Got the police bustin at me, but they can't do nothing to G"

My phone ringing caught me off guard and stopped my turn up session, but not hesitating to grab it I answered, "Hello?" I hated how proper I sounded sometimes. I mean, how educated I sounded. I loved the idea of slang. The ability to make words other words and just having a lingo that couldn't be touched. I loved it, it was rare that I was able to use it, but when I did, I loved it.

"Nigga, don't answer the phone all proper and shit with me." My homeboy Carlos yelled through the receiver.

"Carlos, my man." I laughed. Carlos was my homeboy from childhood. He was a newscaster at Raven's Pointe, major news network. He was like the Steve Harvey of television. He was able to be politically incorrect, unfiltered, and a wild child. I envied him tremendously. "Bruh, I didn't know who it was calling. You know I gotta keep the mask on until I win." It was true. If I won, they would see a different side: an easy going, but slightly aggressive side.

"I feel that, but I called because I saw somebody today. I thought you'd be happy to hear about it." He sang like he had seen the Queen of Sheba.

"Who?" I asked. I had no idea who this nigga was speaking of. There weren't many people that I hadn't seen or none that I couldn't see. Everyone was always around me now. I rarely had a moment to chill. But from the tone in his voice I could tell that whoever it was someone I hadn't seen in a while but may have needed to see.

"Guess man!" Carlos muttered. I knew that mutter it was a female and she was fine, but I had no clue who. His voice dropped more octaves again letting me know that this was someone worth my time and worth his phone call.

"Lisa?" I asked. Lisa was my first, but she wasn't important. And as an adult, she wasn't that fine either: pretty basic and dense. If it was her I'd have to politely decline his trip down memory lane. I'd actually have to get his eyes checked if that's who he was raving about.

"Nope, Rose." He replied. I let the line go silent, "Nigga, she looked like a chocolate sundae that I'd like to pour my syrup on top of. Damn!" He exclaimed. He was saying other shit, but my mind was still stuck on hearing her name, the name I hung onto for many years. The name I secretly said with so much love.

Rose, I thought. Damn, it was like the earth stood still and shattered as I thought of her big beautiful big brown eyes, curvy hips, flat stomach and the richness of her skin. Lawd, as an adult, I'd do some things to her body that would have her climbing the walls and me searching for her with a flash light. I was sure she had blossomed into an even more beautiful person than what she had been years ago.

"What about her?" I asked playing it off. I fucked that up and I knew it, but there was no way I could let on that I still thought of her from time to time. It was Rose, the first girl I met at Ivy University. She was a cool, funny, around the way girl. She said what came to her mind and she enjoyed life. She enjoyed it so much, and at a time I enjoyed watching her enjoy it. I ruined a friendship no a partnership, afraid that she would taint the image I was searching for. We were getting older, and she seemed to be going down a path I couldn't fuck with. So being the stupid obedient person I was back then I cut it off before we even got started. We were meant to be; there was no denying that, but we couldn't be.

"Don't play that bullshit with me, fam. I said fucking Rose. Rose the beauty, Rose with the body of a damn goddess, and Rose that loved your stupid ass even when you didn't fucking deserve it." He reminded.

"Los, she ain't for me dawg." As soon as I said that, I had a notification coming in from him. Putting him on speaker, I opened the picture and my mouth started watering. It was an off-guard photo, her hair was wild and curly, her midriff showed from the crop top she wore, and that ass. She looked good, damn good. She looked so good I wanted to recant all the shit I said moments ago and hunt her down.

"She looking good as fuck ain't she? I saw her at the pub earlier. I wanted to stop and get her number for you, but I said nahh, that stick in the booty ass boy won't know what to do with all that." He laughed. I didn't find shit funny. Carlos was my boy, but he was damn near my hardest critic. He didn't agree with the course my life had taken but he still supported me.

"Why you always playin?" I added.

"Because that fucking stick figure you fuckin' with ain't the gotdamn one. You need to stop playin' ya 'self, all the boys know it, and you know it too."

"You know what I'm trying to do though," I declared a lot less confident than normal. I was tired of explaining to people the shit I was on. I couldn't take everyone with me. Rose was just one of the casualties along the road to triumph. She knew Thorn and that's who she fell for. She didn't know Damien Thorn: the mogul, the future senator. "We not compatible man. Rose would never submit or let me lead."

"Well give me the go ahead, I'll put her pretty ass on my team. It'll be like fucking magnets how strong our connection will be." Los replied in all seriousness. No laugh, no chuckle, and no joke. That made my stomach turn. The thought of him tarnishing something as pure as the rose to my thorn didn't sit right, but I couldn't do anything about it. For now, all I could do was think of the good times and pray some day she forgave me without an apology. My mind wandered to the first day I ever laid eyes on her as Carlos continued to ramble on and on about what he would do to her and how much she had grown up.

"Today, is the day you little spoiled brats learn a lesson on understanding your peers." Professor Lovelace preached with his snarky attitude. I couldn't understand why it was so important for us to learn about the struggle. The idea of college was to overcome the struggle or the possibility of a struggle. Not put us in it to learn some lesson that none of us would even take seriously or remember when life went back to normal.

"Mr. Thorn is there a problem?" I heard him ask. He must have seen the smirk on my face. I really needed to work on my faces if I wanted to take this senator shit my parents wanted seriously. I had a hard time hiding my feelings or my mood, but I had to do better, or it would get me in trouble.

"No sir, it's just that I don't understand why we have to learn about something we didn't come from or plan to never go through."

"Wow!" she bellowed, "Everyone in this room, on this campus, didn't come from a privileged life such as yours. I understand that it's hard to grasp the concept of life being bigger than your immediate circle but look around everyone in this room doesn't look like you or get to wear Gucci loafers, cardigans with them stupid ass toggles you got on. Oh, and let me not forget about your larger than life my dick is little, look at me, look at me, watch." I was caught off guard with her words. If not more caught off guard with her reference to my dick. A dick she knew nothing about. But after the shock of her disrespect and complete humiliation wore off I admired her beauty. Damn this little piece of chocolate that called me out had me ready to show her exactly how big my little dick was. Her hair was so damn curly and pretty. I wanted to touch it, run my hands through it. Her smile, the 'yeah, I just called you out nigga' smile adorned her face was breathtaking.

"Ms. Trulicity thank you for taking the words right out of my mouth." Professor smiled. I found nothing funny about her less than candid use of words to a man, to me. "Mr. Thorn please pick up your face, so we can continue."

Before I could turn back around her juicy glossed lips formed to blow me a kiss. Fuck that kiss. I wouldn't dare give her the time of day. Where I grew up at women were to be seen not heard and the noise she just made wasn't cute, attractive or funny. Men hated when they were laughed at, and I was no different. It was a blow to the ego for a woman to make a joke and it be laughed at by the masses. I was low-key pissed off, but I had something for her ass. I was irresistible and eventually payback would be mine and she would regret that little dick joke when I had her gagging and her back arched to the sky. Yeah, I wasn't even sweating the shit.

"The struggle is important to learn so history doesn't repeat itself. Without pain we wouldn't know pleasure, without sorrow we wouldn't know joy. It's our duty as

43

a society to learn the things that happened so we don't do the same shit as the generation before. I have cooked up a fun project for fall break."

The entire class groaned. African American history was boring, but Professor Lovelace did his best to make it entertaining and thought provoking. I honestly didn't understand why it was here at Ivy, most of the population was white. We had a sprinkle of black people but not enough to teach these fucks about our history. History that they didn't give a fuck about. History that these bastards had a hand in.

"I don't understand why we need to teach these colonizers anything, their family was there and can tell them all about it." Trulicity, as I learned replied to the professor's proposal on his project. She was on a damn roll and I fucked with it hard. As long as it wasn't directed towards me. I didn't want to be at the front of any of her jokes. But from the look on her face it didn't look like she was joking.

"We can't let them continue to tell OUR history, we must show and tell. Not just the white people in our community but those that were born with a silver spoon in their mouth. Unfortunately, the struggle isn't just for African Americans. The struggle knows no race." As the professor walked closer I got a notification. Checking it, I smiled Ashlyn was always hot and ready.

What's up Mr. Mandingo? Let's meet up later.

"Mr. Thorn, please share your text message with us, you know since it was more important that paying attention to my class." I groaned as the professor called me out again.

My body went stiff at the thought of reading the message from Ashlyn. I was beginning to feel like the whole class was against me. Which was hard for me to grasp, everyone loved Thorn. I was the pick of the litter; fuck was he on? Maybe he had a crush on Trulicity or something and was showing off. I wasn't feeling it either way. I didn't appreciate humiliation.

"Come on Mr. Thorn don't be shy." He said placing his hand on my shoulder. I was unnaturally still, my rapid blinking and change in temperature had me

44

searching for the nearest exit. But I didn't, adversity would always be present. I was convinced he was hating on me and attempting to embarrass me. I stood like a man and read the message with pride. Someone was getting some ass, and someone wasn't, that was the issue. His drought wasn't on me. Maybe if he loosened up and wasn't a bore he could get some action.

"What's up, Mr. Mandingo? Let's meet up later." I smiled widely. Shit this was going to work in my favor. It would clear up any misunderstanding of my dick being little with little Ms. Chocolate Drop in the back. As I sat back down the class starting to laugh and the blondes, brunettes laughed and tossed their hair to the side. A clear sign of interest. It was a win for me.

"Class I will be emailing you the details of the project and the due date. Your partner will also be copied and attached. Class dismissed."

Finally! I thought. I was geeked to get the fuck up out of class. Ashlyn was trying Netflix and fuck, it was the weekend and campus life was lit. Life was good. I'd check my email on Monday and figure out what part of the project I had. Hopefully it was just showing up because I was good at that.

"Tru and Mr. Thorn, a moment." I heard as I started to pack up my shit. Sighing and turning to the front I sat back down and watched as Tru made her way to the front. Damn she had body for her age. Her body was uncommon around here and no one but me would know what to do with it.

"I see a lot of potential for the both of you and I think it would be important for you two to be partners. You see Tru here had to scrap and claw her way here and that didn't exonerate her from the struggle. You got lucky, you got here because it was your parents' wishes and they had the resources to make it happen. I think it would be beneficial for you both to get to know each other and be there for one another during your college career. You are both a scarcity in these parts." He preached. I was sick of his shit. My parents had money and resources, but I had a 4.0 GPA, I graduated at the top of my class and I wasn't here because my parents pulled some strings. I was here because I worked just as hard to get here.

45

"With all due respect Professor Lovelace, I wouldn't be caught dead with this fuck-boy ass kissing coon, he would never understand me, and I have no time to teach him how to understand me." She hissed. Damn she was rude as fuck. I don't know what I did to her. I wanted to be offended but it wasn't the first time someone said the shit to me. I learned a long time ago that what I had was being misconstrued with who I was. I loved my people and it didn't matter that I grew up around white people or within their circle. Soon I would be on the front line fighting for them. I let it slide because she didn't know a fucking thing about me.

"When do we start?" I asked. She would know everything about and eating those words by the time I was done with her. I could be down, I made a choice not to be. I wouldn't fight back on the assignment because I knew it would bother her more if I didn't. I would do this assignment with a smile and prove to her that she wanted me and that was why she was acting like a complete bitch.

"Tru I wasn't asking; this assignment is worth half of your grade. Get to it." The professor advised crushing her face and putting mine back together.

"I'm Damien," I said extending my hand. I never backed down from a challenge. She would be feeling me, all of me before summer arrived. I had plans to make her not only fall for me but fall hard for me.

"Tru," she replied shortly not making eye contact and not giving me any indication that she was happy with this arrangement. That was the day I vowed to make something memorable and solidify something between me and her. Now in the present, I realized that I broke a lot of promises to her. Professor Lovelace ended becoming my mentor and he was right about us sticking together. No one on that campus had my back like Rose did at the time. She made sure I stayed on top of my assignments, she made sure none of the skanks trapped me or pinned shit on me. I loved her deeply back then for all that she meant to me.

"Do you, bruh. I know you don't respect guy code." I mumbled. After I said that shit, I felt like a hater, but it was out there in the universe and I couldn't take it back. Carlos didn't deserve a woman on the level of Rose. She wasn't ordinary or your everyday woman. She wasn't some silly broad that took whatever was handed to her. Rose complimented any man she accompanied; she was the root to the tree. Life ended and began with her. Carlos didn't deserve that, friend or not.

"Nah, I wouldn't do that. I think there's hope for you two. I mean all you gotta do is stop living for everyone else, and finally do what Damien wants."

Carlos always said that shit like it was so simple. It wasn't. It wasn't easy saying fuck all the hard work you already put in, the sleepless nights, the long hours at the office, the transformations you completed to finally be viewed as one of them. That wasn't some meek shit, it was heavy. I done and made it to where I was. There was no way I was throwing all away for anyone, not even the rose to my thorn.

"Alright man, I got a long day tomorrow." I said ready to end the call. I couldn't carry the conversation on if he refused to see where I was coming from. Trulicity would always be the one that had my heart, the one that got away, but I couldn't and wouldn't risk it no matter how wide her hips had spread, no matter how smooth her skin was. *Gotdamn Rose*, I thought to myself.

"T, man don't be mad with me. I just want you happy ain't no harm in that."

I couldn't remember the last time I was content. It seemed so long ago that I actually did anything for myself. I didn't even know what I enjoyed anymore. Things had to change, but I had no idea where to start without jeopardizing all that I had gained.

I lived in a half million-dollar condo that I owned, I drove the latest Mercedes, and I had enough shoes and clothes that I never had to wear the same ones twice. I had been around the country once or twice, I dined at the finest restaurants, and I shook hands with some of the most important people in the world. Life for me was made if we

47

calculated by monetary value, but it wasn't supposed to be like this. The value equaled zero without a woman that complimented me on my arm, making me a part of the mile-high club, feeding me food off her fork, making me laugh at her corny jokes or matching my fly. I desired that, but I desired to be powerful and remembered more. The power meant more to me than the thought of love, and now I was too far gone to turn back and find a position in the middle.

"Yeah, I know." I responded. I felt were Los was coming from. I was a man that had lived life for other people long enough. I deserved to make my own decisions and ultimately dictate my own happiness. It should've been on my terms, but the minute I did that, I would lose myself in only that and forget what I was destined for. It was a no go, for now. Maybe in a few years I would focus more on being me, going back to Thorn. Right now, Damien, future senator was my main focus. The only focus.

The sky was clear, and the air was perfect for a walk in the park. The more work I done the more my spirit felt stagnant. Nothing was running through me anymore or maybe it was the latest job I was tasked with. It all felt like a scam and I couldn't shake the feeling of being no better than my counterparts. If I was to bring them information on Damien, I would ultimately be in agreeance that he was undeserving. I knew that to be a lie, but damn, revenge sounded so sweet. But who would I be avenging by stooping so low? My brain was fried and scrambled attempting to sort all this shit out.

To clear my mind, I followed my heart to my favorite spot, the Park on Damascus. It was something about the simplicity of the park that always provided a level of clarity I couldn't find anywhere else. I couldn't find it at home, I couldn't find it at my office and I couldn't find it at my mother's home. This was the spot, this was the only location that allowed me to be honest about my fears, my desires and my shortcomings.

I was still no closer to finding dirt on Thorn than I was when I received the job. I don't know why I was surprised. I knew him well even after the transformation. He would never do anything to jeopardize his livelihood. He was always in control. He knew his limits well, he read vibes well, he did it all well. I wanted to be frustrated that he was making my job way harder than it needed to be, but I wasn't, I felt a sense of pride that he was doing exactly what he has set out to do. I was proud that his eyes were still on the prize. It didn't hurt as much anymore that I had to be kicked to the curb for him to get it. I guess because I was pleased with his progress.

I ran through my mental rolodex of people that I may be able to contact about Thorn and get information on, but I was coming up short. It just so happened the night I was tasked with the job I saw his old friend Carlos, I didn't stop. Carlos had always been one slimy ass nigga with his lingering eyes and handshakes. Plus, he wouldn't have told me shit anyway. They had always been butt buddies, and I knew that hadn't changed. That I was surprised by, why wasn't Carlos cut from the circle like me. Carlos was by no means on the same path or level as Damien. He was loud, obnoxious and loved being the center of attention. That couldn't have been good for his image. Again, I was feeling jaded.

That feeling didn't last long as I heard a young girl's scream for help. I exhaled sharply not in the mood to save the day right now. I had way too much on my mind for someone to need my assistance, but my nature wouldn't allow me to shut it out.

"No, stop," I heard in the distance. I couldn't see where it was coming from, but I stood to my feet and followed the pleas for help.

"Hel— "the last help came out more muffled than I cared for. My skin started to change and the hairs on my body stood at attention. Throwing my hood over my head and stopping to lace my boots I gathered my thoughts and started for the sound.

Rounding the corner at the back parking lot, I see a young girl scantily dressed being drug by two white males. Both in polo shirts, one staggering and the other laughing. *Oh, hell nah,* I said to myself. Not making a sound I carefully lurked until I was in close enough reach to startle and make sure they were unable to run.

"Wow!' I clapped looking from man to man. They were both under the influence that was obvious. It looked like they had plans of having a good night until someone had way too much. "Please tell me you don't plan on taking advantage of this young lady?"

My conversation with captors was always weird, I wanted them to know that I knew what was going on. I wanted them to also be aware that they weren't slick by any means. I was completely aware of the situation.

"Mind your business, freak," the comic screamed my way. I wasn't offended by that term anymore. I'm sure my red rose hue looked creepy. I shrugged.

"Or what?" I asked.

"Or your fucking next."

"Next for what?" I asked.

"Lady, just go away and mind your business. We just want to get our money's worth."

"Oh, so you plan to do what, a struggle snuggle? Rape? Take advantage of a drunk woman?" I quizzed. I swear some men just made you hate the entire race of men. Always taking what they want as if you had no say in it.

"We plan to get our money's worth and if you don't scram you'll be next." He threatened. I laughed hysterically because as always, a man was underestimating me. Without much though I brought his head and slammed it into my knee. Tossing him roughly into the shrubbery near the parking spot I proceeded to address his friend.

"Y'all done ruined my damn moment of silence with your fuckery. Let her go or you'll be next." I warned. He was sweating profusely, looking on with wide eyes and silent. He wasn't as mouthy as his friend. He would try me because he felt it was the right thing to do and because no man wanted to look like a coward running from a girl.

"Go Away," he said swinging a pocket knife.

"You people are so boring; why doesn't anyone ever want to fight with me?" I yawned. Weapons didn't scare, I would break his arm and stab him with his own knife or let him stab me and watch me heal right away. Either way it would be fun to watch him shit on himself in complete disbelief.

"Stupid bitch, I said leave. What are you captain save-a- hoe?"

"I always wanted a superhero name, thanks for that but I'm not going anywhere until you put her down and take this ass whooping you got coming." I replied.

I could see the fear mixed with confusion in his face. This was the moment he weighed his options. Leave his friend or get his ass beat like his friend. I prayed for he went with his first option because I needed to get back to what I was doing before I was so rudely interrupted. He was taking too long to think about his next move, so I made it for him.

Closing my eyes and stretching my hand, I lifted our scantily dressed friend from the ground and made her hover over him. It was a beautiful sight, she looked like an angel floating into the abyss. What seemed to be an ugly situation was now a beautiful one to me. She was out of harm's way and being viewed as the beautiful creature she was meant to be. She was above the pain and self-destruction.

"Are we done here, ,or do you still want to try your luck?" I asked, bringing her closer to me and into my arms.

Like I knew they both would they ran off, leaving me to deal with another individual needing me to get them to safety. I remembered being in college and doing wild shit, but I always had Thorn to protect me and make sure I got to my dorm safely. It pained me that every woman at a young age didn't have a protector and someone to look after them. It also pained me that every waking moment I was now thinking of me and Thorn. All the good times, all the bad times and the times that I wished I had said or done more.

I had to wear some of the blame for how I blew him off and shut him down when shit was getting to close. I'm sure my mixed signals made it easy for him to ignore me and essentially let me down.

"Focus," I said to myself as I carried sleeping beauty to my car. I couldn't leave her in this dark park full of zombie walkers, not in the state she was in and I damn sure wasn't staying here to watch her. My intuition was telling me to find Thorn and do some more spying. But first I had to get rid of the current thorn in my side.

I watched her as we rode in silence, her in the backseat sprawled out me in the front constantly checking my surroundings. Danger didn't scare me, people finding out scared me. I always felt like someone was watching me and my moves. I couldn't confirm it, but I just always got that feeling that someone outside of my small circle knew what I possessed within myself.

"Hhmmm," she moaned. We were close to the hospital and I prayed she wasn't coming to. Her blonde hair was sprawled across her forehead, her skirt was well above the knee and her crop top ripped. I felt a sense of pride that I was able to save her from having her life ruined by two dick heads that didn't understand human principles.

The rape culture was out of hand and I believe it always had been. In college there were many times I had to escort drunk girls that were easy victims back to their dorms. Boys were savages, they preyed on the weak and that I couldn't have. Your style of dress, the way you carried yourself nor the extra shit you got into made it acceptable for people to take what didn't belong to them. That shit drove me crazy.

Looking at her I wondered what her story was. Was she rebelling from her rich family? Was she on a quest for her own liberation and partying on a Wednesday with two assholes was her idea of living her best life. Or had she fallen into the drug crisis and was exchanging sex to fight her habit. Either way she didn't deserve to be taken advantage of.

"Who are you?" I heard her ask from behind me. Looking in my rearview I could see the fog lifting and her returning to herself. I counted to ten waiting for the scream and the name calling but it never came.

"Relax, I'm taking you to a hospital. Do you remember anything from tonight?" I asked.

"No," she said solemnly.

"Well you are safe now, I was in the park when 2 guys attempted to carry you off into the sunset." I joked.

"Uber driver can you just shut up and drive," she said rolling her eyes. Like a bitch hadn't saved her from being touched and ruined.

"Excuse me?" I said. I wished people weren't so weird about shit because I had a lot of good advice and I always had good intentions, but little Miss Molly was about to get read from left to right like a book.

"Just drive the damn car, and I'm not going to the hospital. Take me to Lepers Hall on the 13th ave."

My eyes were crossing from attempting to bite my tongue and keep my rude thoughts to myself. I looked at her in the rearview mirror and she had the nerve to be squeezing her cheeks as if she was still partying.

"Get out," I said pulling over. I was done with this shit and helping for the night. I had done my part she was safe and away from one set of hound dogs, she would be on her own.

"You've been paid," she replied with a snarky attitude, confirming her story. A rich college kid with the world at her finger tips that's rebelling and making stupid decisions she will one day regret.

"You do realize you've been passed out drunk for an hour and someone had to save you from yourself, check your phone and let me know if you find a uber request bitch" I said waiting for her to get the fuck out. This wasn't the stupid shit I signed up for.

"I'm not leaving this car," she yelled kicking the back of my seat. I braced myself for the storm as I removed my seatbelt, opened my door and made my way around the car. This bitch was getting out and she was getting out now. I was also going to tell her hoe ass a thing or two.

Almost snatching the door off the handle from the irritation coursing through my veins, I yelled in her face "Get your funky, spoiled, stupid ass out of my damn car. I'm not your uber or chauffer. I fucking helped you and made sure Matt and Dillon back there didn't rape you or worse kill you. You are welcome. Now get the fuck out and walk since you got it all figured out." I was huffing and puffing like I had ran a hundred-meter dash.

This wasn't my powers talking or taking over this was pain from seeing another young girl going down the wrong path. I couldn't focus on that because she had me so damn mad at her lack of concern for my time and for herself. I grabbed her bag and her shoe from the back seat tossed them on the ground, hopped back in the car and drove off.

"Fuck you" she yelled stomping her foot. As I burned rubber leaving her ass on the side of the road having a fit. For once the privileged couldn't shit on those willing to help. She could call her a real uber that had to take her shit because I was not.

Heading to Bolo wasn't in the plans anymore. I was going home to calm my nerves and get some sleep. This shit could wait, fuck Ryan and his deadline. I was going to do this on my time not his. Driving and too much thinking led me to my favorite place, my mothers. I was going home and spending time with her tomorrow. I deserved it and so did she for always being so understanding.

Invitation to Doom

Waking up at my mother's house felt good, I missed her, I missed my old bed and I missed the smell of something in the crock pot. She was my entire world and not seeing her for a few days was torture. It was rare that I went longer than a few days with speaking or even seeing her, but duty called. Life was getting in the way of my normal practices and it may have been time to slow down. I had been going hard for years trying to make a name for myself. I wasn't sure I was pleased with the payoff because it didn't seem worth it anymore. I lived for a challenge, but this wasn't that anymore, this was insanity.

"Ma," I yelled out coming down the stairs. I smelled food cooking, so I knew today was special. My father Lionel would be home from working on the train and I couldn't wait to hang out with them both. Mom was the sassy one, and my father, he was the sensible one. Both beautiful people inside and out. I loved them both dearly, but I knew they loved me more than life itself. I was lucky enough to be an only child and to grow up with both parents present. I know that was taken for granted but my parents were direct reflections of God's blessings upon his children.

"Ma, I smell peach cobbler!" I yelled again as I walked further into their two-story brick home. It still looked the same as it did when I was growing up. Flower wallpaper on the walls, religious murals adorned the wall, and plastic on the couches. We were classified as middle class. We weren't rich, but we weren't poor. Both parents had to work to make sure everything stayed afloat. We had our good moments, and we had our rough moments. The layoff of 96' was a hard time for us but we made it and God saw fit to bless my father with something better. We knew the struggle but thank God for a praying mother. Through it all, we had each other. We had laughs, we had dance offs, and we had moments that made me want a husband and kids. Watching my father do some of the simplest things made me want a love that was indescribable.

"Back here, Rose" I heard off in the distance. Following her voice, I found my mother and father on the back patio with a glass of lemonade. I sat in my designated patio chair, kicked off my shoes, poured a glass, and sat back to enjoy the quiet. The week had been long and the cases stressful. I declared that next week would be a better week. It had to be. Colleen would be working the normal cases while I started the hunt for dirt on Damien.

"Ma, the flowers look really good this year." I acknowledged. She loved gardening as much as she loved cooking. I was no different, I loved the nurturing gardening allowed me to take part in and the cooking, love came from cooking. It made everything taste better. Any chance I had I was in the kitchen trying a new recipe. I wish I had someone to cook for and let them eat off the spoon but for now work was my man. It was truly tragic but my reality. I dealt with the feeling of loneliness the best way I knew how, mostly by drinking.

"Honey, that flower bed gave me ten tons of shit. I guess this year's freeze pissed it off." She laughed.

"It still looks good, mommy. Daddy, how was the train? Robert piss you off this time?" I looked just like my father, I had his chocolate skin tone, his big eyes, height and thin nose. He was truly my first love. I enjoyed his stories of work. Because I appreciated how humble he was. He started at the bottom, as a switch person and now he was lead technician. I was proud.

"Well you know how it go, sugga. I had some good days and I had some bad ones. But I'm close to retiring, so I take it how they come."

"So wise old man," I smiled. My daddy hung the moon and stars in my world, and I took heed to anything he said. He could tell me no wrong and do me no harm. Since I was a small girl, he always shared his wisdom and made sure he set an example of what I deserved. I had high standards and it was because of my father. It was because of my father that I was single. I just couldn't find anyone that would accept me or the fact that I wasn't like everyone else. I had to hide so much from so many people out fear. Even my parents had no clue about my powers. My mother speculated when something would end up broken, but I never let her imagination become fact. I had to protect them, the working class was already a target. A regular girl having such power would bring the stakes and the judgement. This town would never accept that I had something they didn't.

"You know Damien is in town. I always liked him." My mother said. I rolled my eyes and so did my father. I had no words for him, him being in town or whatever else she would cook up in the name of matchmaking. Damien's shady ass ruined our friendship, not me.

"Well good for him. Have you spoke with Darlene?" I asked although I didn't care. I was just being polite. My mom loved Darlene, and for good reasons. They grew up together same country town in Avia, both rose from the ashes and lived a good life.

"Yeah she invited us over for Sunday dinner. It would be nice for you to come. She asked about you." I cringed watching my mom wink. Her sly smile let me know she still had no clue what happened between me and Damien years ago. When we met, we had no clue our parents knew each other. It wasn't until we came home for the holidays one year that we realized that we had known each other all along. I smiled thinking back to a time I couldn't stand him and thought it was absolutely foolish to be in his company.

"Tru, I came to pick you up, its better if we just ride together." He suggested. Damien always thought he knew what was better for me and I assure you he didn't.

58

Professor Lovelace and his stupid fucking project was giving me a migraine to the tenth degree. The idea of having to take Damien home for the holidays so he could see how the middle class operated was sure to be a catastrophe. And it didn't end there, I had to go and observe how his family operated. I already knew how they operated. Noses in the air, fancy robes, big house with servants most likely family. I didn't need additional information on the snobs, but I couldn't afford to fail a class putting my academic scholarship in jeopardy.

"I plan to take the train, go ahead without me." I responded as he leaned up against the pillar outside my dorm. He was so fucking handsome, and it pissed me off. I didn't want to like him but since this assignment it seemed I couldn't beat him off with an ugly stick. He calls it stuck up I call it un-muthafuckin' interested, but you can't tell the hot commodity and campus whore that. He thinks he is a God and these bitches let him.

"Trulicity, come on, I am not letting you take the train when I'm headed right that way." His eyes pleaded with me to fold and honestly, I didn't want to take the train, but I was feeling as though we needed some space. For the last two weeks we've been attached at the hip, well when he wasn't in between someone else's. It was weird because my mind told me to despise him, but my body betrayed me every time his crisp line up was in sight, his Yves Sain't Laurent cologne was inhaled or those white teeth that caught my attention were around. I could count on him looking and smelling amazing as he walked me to my class or meet me in the library. "What's your problem with me?" he asked. Jarring me out of my inappropriate thoughts.

"Huh?" I asked.

"What's your problem with me, Tru?"

I don't know why I expected him to know. He thought he was the man with the master plan. But to me he was just an annoying, privileged, spoiled man that didn't understand that no matter what he did or how proper he acted he was just like me.

"Nothin', it's just that time of the month." I lied. I couldn't tell him how I really felt. My heart held some hope for him, for us I guess. I don't know what I meant by for us. I knew friends was all we would be when it came down to it. I

59

wasn't his type and I didn't know my type yet. I came to college a virgin even when my mom said it was a bad idea.

"Well get in, it's starting to rain." He smiled opening the door for me.

"Ok fine," that smile could convince me to rob a bank, join a sex ring or anything else he asked of me.

The heat felt good and the leather seats were like memory foam or some shit. I was in heaven as I sat in the luxury vehicle. Yep, Thorn had an older model Mercedes even in college. How could you not feel some type of way about his privilege? I had a hard time separating it and not being pissed with my own family for not having better. This was why we needed space, his life had me for the first-time questioning shit that didn't need to be questioned. I had a wonderful childhood filled with the things that some couldn't purchase. Intangible shit.

"What music you want me to put on?" he asked.

I turned to look at him and the gleam in his eye scared me a little. He hadn't looked at me like this since we started on this project. That gleam was different. It wasn't the smirk I had become accustomed. The sneaky grin that lets you know that a man just had an inappropriate thought about you. This look was of admiration, he liked me enough to get to know me. Too bad I wasn't concerned with getting to know him.

"What Music does Damien listen to?" I quizzed.

"Call me Thorn," he snapped. I take it he hated his name. I loved it. But I also doubted that he knew what his name meant. He wasn't deep like that.

"Why don't you like Damien?" I asked.

"It's the devils name, right?"

"What?" I asked holding my stomach from the laughter escaping. "No silly it means 'to tame'. Your name is perfect 'to tame a thorn' its special." I responded, and I could see his mood shift.

"What's your real name?" he asked putting on some Jodeci.

"Please turn this baby making music off." I didn't know if he was trying to set the mood or what. But I needed something a little more upbeat for this three-hour ride back home. Not something that would have me in my feelings and possibly giving him a blow job while we road on the highway.

"Name?" he asked again.

"Trulicity Rose McCall" I answered looking out the window.

"That's fucking dope, Rose and Thorn. You gotta be the rose to my thorn man." He laughed as Crime Mob played in the background. Now I kind of wanted to hear that baby making music because I think we just had a moment. Oh my God did we just have a moment I thought.

"No!"

"What? Why not?" he screeched merging on to the highway that led us straight to Raven's Pointe.

"Because we are different. You are obnoxious, spoiled and you give off these vibes that I can do without."

"Damn, that was harsh." He played hurt.

I didn't think so, I actually thought it was mild compared to what I could have said and what I've said previously. My thoughts of him were not the nicest or shit I would repeat just yet.

"Well ,I think we would make a great team. That's what this is about anyway right. Us coming together, being a team."

"I suppose but you know like I know that we are so different that it would be a mess. You have your friends and I have mine. Let's just leave it like it is."

"Rose, I didn't ask you to marry me."

He just called me Rose as if he was my bestie. This was why I didn't want to tell him my name in the first place. It was personal, and I wasn't sure if he was worthy of any personal information. I mean taking him home to meet momma was personal enough.

"I wouldn't if you asked." I stated matter of factly. That shut him up. Out the corner of my eye I watched his jaw flinch. Little Damien couldn't fathom the idea of someone not throwing themselves at his feet. It tickled my soul to cut him down to size. Watching his slender hand turn the radio up I reclined back and jammed to Lil Kim as he sat silently brewing.

"I even dig yo' man's style, but I love yo' profile

Whisper in your ear and get you all shook up

But don't blush, just keep this on the hush."

Rose for the WIN, I cheered on in my head. The rest of the ride was silent until we pulled up to my childhood home two hours later. Turning in my seat I explained what to do and not to do. "We aren't dating, we aren't friends, this is for a project."

"I know; trust me I don't want to be here no more than you do." He responded without making eye contact. He was upset.

Wow I thought to myself. How rude was that? I know we didn't have a big iron gate, servants meeting at the door or expensive shrubbery, but our home wasn't too shabby. But instead of standing in 40-degree weather I proceeded to the front with him close on my tail.

"Rose!" my mother squealed opening the door. It was as if she was anticipating my arrival or looking out the window. "Damien, it's been so long. How are you?" she asked.

Snapping my neck around I was confused, "You know him?"

"Mrs. McCall it's been way too long." He replied. My head was swiveling like a bobble head attempting to make sense of all this.

"Someone, please explain what's going on." I shouted a little louder than I should have or even meant to.

"Rose, chill." He coached as my mom led him further into the home. It felt tainted at this point. So much for vacation I thought.

That was the day I realized I knew Damien or of Damien way before college. Our parents went way back and by the time Damien was four, Mr. Thorn has secured his spot in town as the mayor. Our families became distant, which was normal for a family with status now. The minions couldn't come, and it pissed me off that my mom still considered Darlene a friend. The Christmas gifts, and sporadic calls didn't solidify friendship. But Shantay didn't see it that way.

From that point we were stuck like glue. Interacting with him and seeing how much my father admired him made me feel something inside, that I wasn't sure of. I didn't know how to process that I finally had him, the one and only Thorn as a friend. After realizing that we knew each other our energy changed. It was like we were two magnets that couldn't part. The jokes of it being fate were moments that we laughed at and I took seriously, and he didn't.

"Ma, I'll probably be working on something. Send my love." I responded. That trip down memory lane was the one thing I wanted to avoid. I was strong, but not strong enough to match what we shared at one point.

"Rose, I normally don't bother you because you are a grown consenting adult, but I wish for just once you would stop acting like those people did something to you. Not to mention you owe me, remember?" She fussed. She was so naïve, to Darlene's bullshit. I wish she was just purposely overlooking her flaws, but I knew she truly felt Darlene and her were one in the same. She couldn't have been more wrong.

63

"I seriously don't want to deal and be fake. And really momma, you don't have anything else you want me to do." My mom looked disappointed and let's just say I didn't care. I wouldn't tell her that, but I didn't. In fact, they had done something to me. They made Damien feel like I wasn't good enough for him so how was I supposed to go to their home and pretend that everything was all good.

"Rose, I ain't askin' this time. You will show up and you will play nice or you deal with me."

"Fine Mom, what time? What's the dress code? I'm sure my boots aren't fit for the Queen's palace." I said sarcastically. This would work in my favor. It would allow me to get close to him without having to do much work. Hopefully, he would see me and want to catch up or something. I had no clue, but I would play nice to get what I needed.

"Don't fine mom me, that woman has been nice to you each time she's seen you." Darlene was a fake and a fraud. She never really cared for me as I for her. All that grandiose living made me itch. And of course, she was nice to me when she seen me, she had to save face. It was the shit she did behind closed doors that fucked with me and turned me off.

"Well Mom, she's the first lady, it's her job. I said I'll be there; I'll even do my hair for a change." I was ready to vomit thinking about wearing a dress and actually doing something to my wild and free hair. But for the sake of winning the game that we were secretly playing, I would.

"Meet me here at three, and don't be late. We leave at three thirty."

"Why can't I drive my own car?" I didn't want to ride with my parents like some child. I had a car that was perfectly capable of making it to Boloro. I wanted to tell my mom that I knew how to get there because I was there a few nights ago preparing to blow the top of this little charade but I didn't.

64

"Tru, you know why, you will come eat those people's food and abruptly leave." My mom laughed. She was absolutely correct, but still, I could drive myself. Who cared about their feelings? I surely didn't.

"Fine, I have some shopping to do. Call me later." With that, I left and made my way to my favorite boutique. I had to find something that wasn't saying "Hey pick me" but it couldn't say "Hey, look past me" it had to say "Wow, it's been a minute." I wouldn't do black. I had black everything. I needed something unlike, anything I owned. I needed something that would make his mouth water at fir

Still Changing

Arriving at Uncharted, I immediately entered and looked around. For the first moments, I couldn't believe I was doing this. I was technically doing the same thing he wanted me to do all those years ago, change. It didn't feel good, but you had no idea of the shit I did in the name of a dollar and in the name of winning.

Shrugging, I continued to browse the racks until I found this beautiful white short sleeved wrap dress. It was beautiful. It was completely different from what I normally wore.

"Hey, chika." I heard from behind me.

"I'm so glad you came to help me," I grumbled. I hated shopping. Colleen in true best friend fashion had shown up to save the day. She was the feminine one and she could help fine tune my appearance and hopefully my attitude.

"Miss you in a dress? I wouldn't dare." She laughed.

"I've been summoned at the Thorn Residence, and I can't show up in leather, blue jeans, and boots or my mom will have a fit."

"For? And don't tell me you are dressing up for that low-down flea infested dog Thorn?"

"Not really, but sort of. I'm tired of being seen as some tom-boy hard ass. I can be soft. I can clean up." It sounded so dumb coming out of my mouth. Of course, I wanted to look good when I saw Damien for the first time in years.

"Tru, there's nothing wrong with who you are or the way you are."

"I know but let's just say it's for the job." I sighed, heading to the dressing room, I quickly undressed and slid the dress on. It fit like a glove and flowed so perfectly. Even my curls complimented the dress.

66

I decided right then I would keep them somewhat unruly for the dinner. Stepping out of the dressing room I did a twirl for Colleen who had the look of disappointment in her face.

"You hate it?" I asked.

"No, I love it, but I don't think Damien deserves any of this."

"You might be right but what other choice do I have?" she knew her brother was impossible. I had to do this to get closer, make my mom happy and have free dinner in the process.

"Ryan is not willing to let me work this assignment. So, I guess you are right. But he's always been undeserving of the chance to change you. That hasn't changed in my opinion."

"But I can get closer to Damien with ease. I can ear hustle and find out what people are saying behind his back."

"Any angles yet?" she asked breezing past me getting closer.

"He's seeing someone; I think she may be the way to go or as always follow the money."

"Be careful, and you know Ryan is making you do this because you don't want to."

I knew that was true because that's just the type of asshole he was. But I would show him a thing or two about me. I could make any situation work for my benefit.

"Jokes on him." I said heading back in the dress room. I had no real plan. Which would bite me in the ass in the end. I was going in blindly. Most of my cases were fueled from all the same things. Greed, jealousy, cheating or emotions. But if I could get Damien alone and pick his brain this wouldn't be so bad after all. My biggest fear was seeing him and looking desperate. I prayed I could see Damien and not look at him with regrets, it was his loss after all.

Checking out, me and Colleen decided to go get pedicures and make it a self-care day. I did that every so often. I wasn't a complete boy. I was still feminine but confident. I didn't let myself go, I took care of me. I had to since I had been single since that little fling with Khalil.

"Khalil's been sniffing around," she said with a smirk. I didn't know why she was team Khalil, but she would be on that team on her own. I jumped off the love train a long time ago and I didn't see myself getting back on anytime soon.

"That's what dogs do," I said flipping the page in the newspaper.

"Khalil is nice, established and let's not forget good looking."

"Well you date him!" I was completely engrossed with the article I had just come across in the newspaper. It was an interview of Damien and his goals as senator. Secretly, I was proud. This was what he always wanted to make a change. After our project ended he changed a bit. His view on the world and the struggles of the middle class jolted him to start reaching out and doing more for people that looked like him but that didn't grow up like him. This article let me know he was still on the same path.

"Rose, you know I love you like a sister but it's time for us to settle down and Khalil wants that too. He's always talking to Ryan about you and how he messed up a good thing. I think you should give it a shot. "

"Nope, let's go."

"He was your first love for god's sake," she screamed stopping me from leaving. I rolled my eyes at her and her tricks.

"Sis, Khalil was my first fuck not my first love, I think you get that confused." I responded. Everyone wasn't head over heels for their first. I certainly wasn't. I didn't sleep with Khalil out of love, I slept with him to get rid of the V -card and then after that I slept with him out of convenience. Love was nowhere to be found when I gave it up to Khalil. Khalil, on the other hand took that shit way too seriously. He thought it gave him some sort of special access to my emotionally unavailable vagina and it didn't.

"You are tripping Tru," she mentioned shaking her head. I didn't expect her to understand why, but I did expect her to respect my decision and leave it alone.

"Maybe,"

I settled on nude nails and toes, I got waxed and even bought some new makeup. I was going to wow someone, may not be Damien but someone would be in for a treat. And that person was me. I loved channeling and trying new things. It kept the job fresh. Private investigation was more than snapping photos, you had to be clever, you had to be sly and you had to be quick. It was a task and I think that was why I enjoyed it so much. It left me fulfilled more than anything in the world. □

□

Lonely Nights

Reaching my penthouse, I unlocked the door, greeted Whiskers, my snow paw Siamese cat and proceeded to get everything situated for Sunday. I needed to make sure I was well rested and well versed on the happenings of the rich. Damien was always good at debating and banter and I needed to be in tip top shape.

"Whiskers, what do you think he will say when he sees me?"

"Meow."

"Yeah, I think so too." I laughed. Had my life been reduced to talking to my cat. I needed to get out more. But I had to be careful. When I first realized my powers, it was strange. I had strength, but I was weak to that same strength. I went through moments of misusing those powers. I didn't understand how they worked at first. I would see an opportunity to use my strength and do just that. Not thinking about the consequences or that the news would report on it the next morning. It was probably not the best idea to give a college student power like that. I robbed ATM's before, I stole booze, I stole clothes and other things that I wasn't proud of. I was glad that I moved past that point, my momma didn't raise me like that and she would've beat my ass had she known the things I did. Like that one time I scared the shit out of some frat boys.

"Aye, Mama," a young man howled as I strolled down the avenue. I don't know how he knew I was a woman. My hood was up, my black boots were laced up and my hair tucked. I looked like a robber of some sort. I sped up my pace. My powers were starting to take control of me instead of me controlling them. It was all bad.

"Aye, you deaf?" he continued to scream now turning around to walk up on me. The ringing in my ears started to get louder and louder. I attempted to move faster but the ringing, the shaking of my hands, the red hue from my skin caused him to grab my shoulder and spin me around.

70

"Fucking weirdo," he laughed with his buddy's as if I was some joke. Embarrassment made the rage build and ultimately made me make mistakes that I would have to worry about later. I hadn't got caught yet but the images and the things I did replayed and kept me up at night.

"Don't touch me and I won't touch you," I mumbled attempting to walk away and continue to my dorm he scooted over blocking me. I moved to the other side seriously making one last attempt to control the situation. I looked around because I couldn't afford to be on the news again.

"Where'd you come from out of space?"

"If you know what's best you'd move!" I warned.

"What?" he asked.

"I said MOVE!" pushing his 250-pound body through the front window of his frat house was light work and light weight. I hated shit getting physical but when a lady said cut the shit you should cut the shit. It was disgusting the way men carried on and how they attempted to take advantage.

"Oh, you're a feisty one." Another one grinned.

"Leave me alone please" I ordered. I didn't want to fight tonight. My eyes and body were glowing red, my veins were bulging, and my hands were tough as nails. This would end badly, and I could sense it. His ego however wouldn't let him care.

"Oh no we need payment for that window you broke. We take pussy, head and well more pussy." He responded

I growled at his disrespect. He began to charge at me I grounded myself and flew into the air on top of house. I could stay up here all night and look at the stars. But instead I watched them with a smirk on my face.

"How? What?" they asked.

71

I laughed because now wasn't the time to ask questions. "I told you to leave well enough alone, now bow!" I ordered. Like puppets the men in the yard kneeled in amazement. "Close your eyes."

"Yes, yes ma'am," they stuttered.

I felt powerful watching five men that looked like they could bench press me fall down in surrender. That was the day I realized just how much power I possessed if provoked. Thinking of the things I did back then caused a giggle to escape my lips as I soaked in the tub. I was so reckless and compulsive.

Studying the file Ryan provided I felt like this was a waste. I hadn't learned much more than what I already knew. Well nothing of importance. His career wasn't important. All the dinners, prizes and bullshit he had won over the years wasn't important. I had to dig deeper and look past the obvious. I had to see past the black and white print. I had to read between the lines until I found something that didn't make sense to me but seemed legit to everyone else.

Sipping my glass of wine and soaking it hit me. Erica. There was a reason why Erica had to be the one. I needed to do some research on her. She was the out or the in, however you wanted to look at it. There were several prominent families from Raven's Pointe so for them to pick her was odd. Damien was a democrat and her family was clearly the popular republican family. I could tell by the red everything she owned. People always assumed they were so inconspicuous, but they weren't. Most made careless mistakes, without even trying.

"Erica, what is it about you? Whatever you do, wherever you go Tru will find you," I sang. It was a running joke at the office. I didn't mean to toot my own horn but there was no one in town better at this shit than me. I took risk to close my cases, I didn't sleep until I closed my case, it became my life as it had yours. The worrying and stress became my problem.

Hopping from the tub, I ran to load my computer while I applied moisturizer and pineapple my hair. Stopping, I stared in the mirror at my scars. The scars served as a painful memory of laying in Ryan's sterile lab and being injected with rounds of viruses, that ultimately forced my body to react. I had rashes, cold sweats, sensitivity and moment where I thought I would die.

I had to learn the hard way and the many scars on my back and arms showed the signs of the change happening in me. I was a beast at first, ripping handles off doors, breaking glass doors, and a list of other shit I had no control over. Now, I would call myself a gentle beast. I use my powers for good as often as I can. My courage was activated by compassion. I had to gain control and find a way to make it useful to society. It was safer that way. I appreciated safe although I live a dangerous life. I just do my best at blending in.

Logging on to my portal I compiled all the information I could on Erica Renee Wainwright. "Erica, what is it about you? Whatever you do, wherever you go Tru will find you," I sang again.

Gaining access to her financial accounts was a piece of cake. Scrolling I wasn't surprised by all the superficial shit she purchased from time to time. I wasn't looking for that I was looking for large sums of money being moved or transferred around. Moving on from the recent transactions I browsed around in the scheduled transfers, "Bingo" I yelled grabbing Whiskers. Fifty-thousand dollars was being transferred every three months to the same account. Jotting the account down on a piece a paper I decided to call it a night and get back to it Monday.

Sunday Dinner

Pulling up to the Thorn estate felt like torture, the heels I wore were hurting my feet and my hair had become a big poof due to the morning rain. It looked like a Bernstein bear, total contrast of the elegant dress I wore. Of course, mom fussed about my hair, but time had run out for fixing it. They would get whatever hair that walked through the door. And I dared someone to check me about it.

"Be on your best behavior. Ya' hear?" My mom said. She was going overboard with this act. She had on her best Sunday attire, and my father's sentiment and face matched my own, already over the shit show. But both of us would do anything for her and she knew it.

"I'm an adult. I know how to behave and politic with the upper class. No worries, ma" she wasn't about to work my nerves and act like I had no home training. I would be on my best behavior as long as everyone else was on their best behavior. I wouldn't be disrespected or treated like a peasant. Not today and not ever.

As we ascended the hill of the driveway, cars littered the circle and my nerves were starting to get the best of me. I was under the impression that this would be something intimate with two families that had been friends for years, but no, this looked like a dinner party of some sort. Wondering what we were walking into made my rage start to bubble. *This isn't good* I thought to myself.

Before I could turn on my heels, I heard Darlene's uppity snotty voice, "Shantay, come give me a hug, darling. You look absolutely stunning today." I wanted to pull that tired lace front from her head. My mother looked good all the time. This wasn't some fancy getup to impress her, but I kept my filthy mouth shut. I loved my mother enough not to embarrass her. "Lionel, Dewayne is in the back, doing what men do."

Coming in closer, I could hear the fake laughs and cackling from all the patrons. They were laughing like there was an episode of Martin playing. Without effort my mind went in search of Damien. I was here now and there was no need in acting as if I wasn't excited to see him up close and personal.

"Rose, you have grown up so much. You are breathtaking." She complimented.

I grinned, "Thank you, Darlene. Still fancy and still jeweled out, I see."

I had no real compliment for Darlene. She looked like a punching bag: tight and shiny faced. Yes, Darlene had punch face. I disliked her because she never truly cared for me. It was her, I'm sure, that forced Damien's hand with his choice of spouse, which was odd. I mean, Darlene was a black woman that didn't want her son with a black woman. It was a twist that had yet to be untwisted.

"Oh, you know diamonds are truly a girl's best friend." She laughed a hearty laugh.

"Where's the bar?" I asked. I couldn't handle this dry. I needed a drink, something stiff and horrible tasting to play nice for a few hours.

"In the back corner, dear. Enjoy yourself while I steal my bestie."

"Have at it. Mom, I'll be in the back or on the deck if you need me." I loved the outdoors. I did my best thinking when I had a moment to enjoy the sun on my face, and the wind in my hair. The sky was mind freeing. The outdoors reminded you that peace was still. I needed still sometimes.

"Fireball on the rocks." I requested from the bar. What Sunday dinner had an open bar? "So extra," I said shaking my head, attempting to shake the annoyance surfacing.

"Still a fireball drinker, huh?" his strong voice stopped me in mid grab. The hair on my arms stood and I had visible chills. Damn, I thought I would be stronger than this. Regaining my composure, I grabbed my drink and turned with the brightest smile, "Damien."

"Rose."

"It's Tru," I responded holding my hand out. We weren't doing this, not here. He wouldn't be able to call me by my nickname as if we were friends and didn't have bad blood between us. The bad blood was still fresh and would be that way until I felt he was ready to give up the lie he lived. At some point, I wanted to forgive him but today wasn't the day. I had to keep the energy for many moons ago in order to complete the job before me.

"Excuse me, Tru. How have you been?" he smiled.

He had punch face too, but I couldn't do that without breaking his nose or pushing his face in. Instead of punching him, I smiled again. Smiling was better than growling right? The said it took more muscles to frown than it did to smile. He would be seeing crow's feet with Ms. Erica and I'd come to remind how black didn't crack. I would laugh at myself, but my jaws were starting to ache.

"I can't complain" I said with a twirl. I looked good and I knew it and by the look in his eyes he knew it too, "How are you?"

"Running for senator," he replied. In that instant, I felt bad for him. He didn't even know how to kick back and be honest or discuss something other than his next notch in the belt.

"I said 'how are you doing' not 'what are you doing'." I had to bring him back. I felt my savior complex kicking in. He needed to be saved from this circus he was in. I could always read him well. The look in his eyes went from surprise to distant to business within seconds. Damn he was already fucked, and I would be fucking him more sooner than later.

"I can't complain Tru, just trying to figure it all out. What are you up to these days?"

"Nothing major, just running my own CI firm and doing as Shantay says." I rarely told people what the true nature of my business was. It caused people to be weird with me. I didn't like to be involved in forced conversations because they were worried about if I was fishing for information. But without even saying my real occupation, the conversation felt forced. I wasn't feeling it and was about to move around at any second.

"Dame, my love. Who do we have here?" she asked looking at me like she had seen a ghost. That confused me. I had never meet this lady before. Her screechy voice made me want to snatch out her jugular. It was annoying, and that old played out ass perfume she had on was too. But he smiled and threw his arm over her shoulder. It was a sign, but I wasn't catching it. Screw them both.

"This is an old friend of mine, Tru McCall. Tru, meet Erica Wainwright, my fiancé." He smirked. I thought about being a jerk and knocking that smirk off his face, but I decided against it, as I sized her up. I wasn't looking to be his fiancé; the smirk was unnecessary. Him having a fiancé wasn't the sign of making it. They would love him in his face and be talking shit behind his back. They would disown him the minute he got out of line. There was nothing to brag about.

"Nice to meet you, honey. I thought I met all your friends," she replied with a tight smile. She sucked at poker faces, that I could tell. She wasn't happy about me being here. But why lie? Females were pressed, bothered and catty, and I had no desire to be a part of an awkward conversation. If she felt threatened she was wrong. I was no threat to the happy picture they were both attempting to paint.

"I'm not important, and I'm no friend. Enjoy yourselves. Damien, it was nice seeing you again. Good luck." I responded. I wanted her to know that the word friend meant nothing to me. We were and would always be more than friends. He let me down, but I still felt the blast of vigor around him. But seeing his face and the robot he had become felt like it had all been a mistake.

"Give me strength," I mumbled as I headed out the back door. It was time to find solace on the deck. His behavior was heartbreaking. The once full of life college student that had the same dreams I had was now stuck in a twilight zone. *Poor Damien,* I thought as I found a comfortable spot on the deck. The sun was setting, and it was perfect.

Pleasant Surprise

Damn, Rose had filled out, more so than what she was in college. The track body was still present, and that quick draw mouth was still running rapid. I used to love how eloquently she would read someone. Her reads were one for the books, and this reminded me of the reasons we weren't compatible. She lacked the poise to be a first lady, she would never allow strangers in our home or entertain them to see me on top.

Truly, she didn't have to, I always felt on top with her. The trip back home solidified our friendship. From that moment we were devoted to building a friendship. I often thought about the good times we shared. Like now, my mind drifted to her and the night the frequency changed within our friendship.

"Rose, let me slide through," I spoke into the phone. I knew I didn't have to ask but one thing about my Rose is that she respected boundaries and she made you respect them as well. Since becoming friends, we had learned the limits of each other.

"For what Thorn?" she asked with an attitude. That made me want to come more. Something was wrong. She was never short with me. We had a bond now, a bond that couldn't be broken.

"I want to chill with you before I go to this party,"

"Thorn, when do you ever have time to study?" she asked.

"I study with you all the time," I said. She was tripping. I was doing just fine in school. Thanks to her and all her help. College had been a fun ride. I was finally able to be myself and not who my parents wanted me to be. I had Rose to thank for

that. She never let me conform or be who they wanted me to be. Her teachings of living my best life stuck with me.

"Fine, I'm cooking so just come in," she responded as I was opening her door. It was quiet, Colleen must have been gone doing hoe shit. I didn't care for Colleen, but she was a part of the clique. Me, Colleen, Rose, Ryan, and Khalil all came from the same place, so it made sense for us to hook up and watch out for each other.

Rounding the corner, I watched Rose stir what smelled like potatoes and her ass was moving right along with the blender. Damn! It was weird because I didn't look at her like that anymore. I mean once I found out that we grew up together and our families were connected it was like she was a sister or something. However, the way she was looking right now in her too little shorts and sports bra was just wrong. Her smooth, clear skin poured endlessly. Her hair was what I loved the most, it was always uninhabited and unrestricted. It looked so good on her. The curve of her back that lead down to her jiggling ass had me adjusting myself and wanting to tear my eyes away, but I couldn't. I couldn't stop staring at my best friend. I couldn't resist the urge to touch her smooth chocolate skin. Her skin on my skin sounded like a good idea. We could make magic.

Moving closer to her quietly and slowly. I pushed her up against the counter, wrapped my arms around her waist and whispered, "I can skip the party,"

"Ahhh" she screeched. "Thorn how long you been here you creep?" she asked holding her chest.

I didn't move, my mind was made up. I had to have her tonight. Fuck the party, fuck the bitch I was seeing and fuck a friendship. I probably knew all along that this would happen. Rose was irresistible, and there was no one like her at Ivy. She was black, intelligent and so damn gorgeous.

"What's wrong with you?" she asked. In my mind I said you being in this house alone with these little bitty ass shorts on, ass moving and shaking. But instead I replied, "Nothing, I'm chilling with you tonight." Backing myself up I leaned on the counter opposite of her and waited for her to turn around.

"You sure?" she asked eyes wide.

"Of course, fuck that party." Those words fell from my mouth and clearly warmed her heart. She lit up like a Christmas tree at the idea of spending time with me. My heart tightened as I felt the shift in the room and also with us. "Make me a plate too."

That night I realized how easily it was for me to miss the signs of what Rose wanted. I could still see how her eyes lit up that night. My thoughts were conflicted now that I had laid eyes on her again. Her hair and that sweet smell that radiated off her body no matter what time of day it was had me hooked, like a fish on a line. She looked amazing in her white dress. It was different, and it made me wonder if she was different or was this just for the moment. I could never tell with Tru; she was one of those women that could do anything. She didn't fit in a box. I couldn't pinpoint one thing about her that would fit and not run into anything else. She was tender, but strong. She was funny but dark, she was down but a runner. She made no sense and that was the thorn to the rose with her.

"Damien, I don't think your friend likes me very much. Did I say something wrong?" Erica loved to play dumb and I hated it. She was the smartest dumb mufucka I knew. I was a man and knew exactly what that was about. And in true Rose form, she made it clear that she was unbothered and that bothered bitches heavily.

"Erica, you good." I had no time to play fuck fuck games with her. Her spot was secure with me. She didn't need to do anything to prove that to anyone else. It was already settled; she was the one that would become Mrs. Thorn. I wasn't proud of the decision, but it was made. It was what would bridge two feuding families together and secure a spot in the house no matter who won.

"You know how I get sometimes. You are so handsome, and any woman would be lucky to have you. I just had to make my presence known," she cooed in my ear. I barely heard anything she said as I watched Tru sit on the back deck in pure bliss.

"Well, it looked like you were making a fool of yourself, it's not needed. I thought we had an understanding?" I had to make sure she remembered that this would never be what she thought it was. No matter how hard she tried, it would be nothing more than an agreement with the occasional fucking involved.

"Yes, of course, but I won't allow you to embarrass me around family. In public, we have to make it seem real."

"Aight" I said walking off and heading to the back deck. I was feeling antsy and completely ready to call this shit off. Damn you, Rose. My mother left this part out and I couldn't understand why. She hated Rose. So why wouldn't she tell me she invited her. Why would she invite her? I know Shantay wasn't the reason. She had been over several times without Tru over the years.

"Still enjoy the sunset too?" I asked stepping onto the back deck. We were alone, just us how it always should have been. It was like a gush of all the memories we had come rushing to my heart. She was doing that thing she always did to me, ignore me if she was upset with me. It had been years and I thought we would've moved past that sad night. "Rose, don't shut me out."

"I've said it already, for you, it's Tru. You don't get to call me Rose, and for the record, I'm not shutting you out. I can't shut you out if you were never in."

That stung a little, I thought she was feeling what I was feeling. I thought she was out here reminiscing on the good times, the laughs and the very close moments. We almost had something solid.

"I was in and you know it," I responded scooting the patio chair closer, we needed privacy, "I know what I did was so fucked up, but I apologize for how I handled you."

"Handled me?" she hissed, "You didn't handle me, you disappointed me. I cared a great deal about you and treated me like I was beneath you. I was a dirty, nasty unworthy black girl. Don't minimize what you did to me, I know. I remember."

Those words nipped at my heart, because I never meant to come off like that. It was a moment of temporary irrationality ending things the way I did. The silly part about it all; we never had anything official. It was almost like what we had was just understood, we didn't need labels. We hung out tough and a few moments we came close, real close to crossing the line. "I cared for you too, I just knew we were headed in the wrong direction, and I had to steer us back in the right path."

"Save your apology Damien, I'm over it. I've moved on and I see you have too, good luck with that."

Watching her walk back in the house was like watching my best friend walk out of my life for a second time, only this time I had no one forcing me to allow her to walk away. It was a beautiful sight watching her ass move from left to right but damn I ruined it again. She was down for me and I cut that off for something I didn't even know if I wanted anymore.

"Honey, it's time for dinner," Erica said miraculously appearing.

"Coming," I replied still trying to pick my face up off the ground. I don't know why I assumed she would accept that half ass apology. I wasn't prepared for this run in and it showed. I was a man that planned and hated spontaneous shit. Seeing her threw me off and knocked me off my square. Tossing back the last sip of Brandy, I made the awkward trek to the dining area.

Finding my spot, it was like my mom was tormenting me, on my right was Tru and on my left was Erica. Why would she put them so close and me in the middle? If this was a test, I'd be leaving tonight with a big F on my paper. I wouldn't be able to control myself around Tru and Erica. Man, she will start that cooing shit she do when other women are around. She wasn't confident like Tru, she would sweat the smallest shit and make it more than what it was. I don't know why I was comparing the two. I knew they were different.

"Ma, can I chat with you for a moment?" I had to know what was up with the seating arrangement. This shit was for the birds. I didn't want to be caught in the middle of my old thing and I guess my new thing. Fuck!

"Son, Rose agreed to come at the last minute." She said before I got the question out. She knew she was on some straight bullshit right now. "I had to put her somewhere. What's the problem?" she asked like she had no damn clue.

"Nothing, it's cool." Walking off, her voice halted me.

"I know you still don't have a love jones for that little girl. Son we talked about this, you just can't if you want to succeed." Whenever she tossed that word around it was like bait. Why was my success contingent on who I had on my arm at the gala, or who I decided to spend my down time with?

"It's fine mom, I just thought it was a mistake. Let's eat," It was useless speaking with her; it was clear this was a test. She wanted to know if I was done with my thoughts or feelings for Rose before I embarrassed my family by fucking over Erica. It confused me a little. It made me feel like my mom had once experienced true love and had to let it go. I felt bad but needed to know more. Until then, I would take my seat and pray the rest of the night went well.

Pissing Contest

By the time dinner was set to take place, I zoned out. The loud classical music, the fake grins and greetings and then him, Damien. His half thought, and half delivered apology was the main source of my vexation. What made him think he owed me an apology after all these years? It wouldn't change a thing. It wouldn't change the words I still heard when I looked in the mirror, and it wouldn't fulfill the dream I once had of being Mrs. Thorn. His apology was hit-or-miss and seemingly purposeless.

"Hey Baby girl, enjoying yourself?" my dad asked on the other side of me. He could sense the brewing going on, I'm sure my temples were sweating, and lip was quivering. My daddy always knew when something was wrong with me, he was an attentive man like that. I would never find anyone like him and that worried me.

"Not really," I whispered. I couldn't risk Damien hearing me complain about his mother's renaissance party. All that was missing was pantalets, bouffant hair, and guest arriving on horses. I was bored out of my mind.

"Me neither, I don't know why we had to be dragged to this damn thing. Ain't not one forty in sight," my father joked.

Chuckling together, I was glad he came and glad he was my neighbor. I loathed how my mother performed around these people. The soulful, funny, down to earth woman I loved didn't exist around Darlene or any of her uppity friends. But my dad, he normally snuck a flask of the good shit we liked to drink, and he normally kept me entertained with making fun of the patrons.

"I think it's time for a troll session, dad," I thought cracking Erica's face would be the highlight of my night but no this would. My father pretending he was in the minds of others would be great.

"I think you're right." He grinned a sly grin. "Look over there with the black blazer, and high waters," looking in that direction imagine my surprise that it was none other than Ryan standing there looking like the bitch ass he was. "That man right there looks like he's got a thumb up his ass."

"Yeah, well check your six," dad's head swiveled slyly "She looks like she's got on a shitty diaper," I laughed. Enjoyment at others expense was our favorite past time and how we bonded.

"Uh oh, it's time for the big pissing contest, ladies and gentlemen pull your dicks out and let us see who has the biggest," he joked sounding like an announcer. I laughed hysterically, as the servers started bringing the plates out in bouffant hair and renaissance attire.

"Dad, stop. I'm going to pee myself" he was in a fit of laughter same as I. Rocking in the chair to stifle my laugh, I caught Erica looking at me like she wanted to fight. Why was Erica staring at me behind Damien's back? She was staring so hard I'm sure she was searching for an imperfection that she wouldn't find. My makeup was flawless tonight, although light. Unlike her, I didn't have to hide the crow's feet surrounding my eyes. She looked at least 45 years old tonight with her Kentucky Derby hat and floral print dress. It was hard to admit but she was the right pick for Damien. I wouldn't be caught dead in a floral print dress. She looked like your grandmother's favorite curtains. It was such a shame, the way the rich carried on. Purchased shit I couldn't dare pronounce for it to be ugly as hell. That caused me to laugh out loud directly in her face.

"What's funny? Care to share?" she asked unaware that I enjoyed a fair game of bullshit.

"Oh, you wouldn't understand." I replied. Scratching my temple with my middle finger. I wanted to tell her to fuck off, they didn't have to be apart or involved in everything, dammit, "It was something from college," Knowing that this would pique her interest. It worked as her barely their eyebrow raised. I could tell that she wanted a reaction and on any other day I'd be happy to oblige, but I didn't break promises to my momma.

"Please share, this party is so drab," she whispered. Her ocean blue eyes couldn't hide the envy brewing inside of her. The reasons remaining unknown. I had nothing that she should desire at all. She had Damien, she had wealth, she had a social life and she was white. But as I thought of it more, she envied my freeness. She envied the fact that I didn't have to do anything for show, I wasn't required to impress people and I damn sure didn't have to marry for status.

"Oh, it's nothing. Just a daddy, daughter moment." Turning and ultimately ending the conversation. He looks and starts with me. He was pissing me off with all this catching up he was trying to do. You had your chance to be a part of the greatness, and you missed the bus. Get over it, already.

"What you been up to lately? Solve any crimes?" he asked, attempting to play nice.

"Just living life, my best life." I wanted him to regret the day he attempted to finish me and the thoughts of myself. I had lived a splendid life without him, and he needed to know it.

"That's good news, I always knew you would make it."

That caught my attention, Damien knew nothing about me. Not the new me, not the confident me, and certainly not the powerful me. I was becoming offended with him pretending that our history didn't get shattered and never put back together years ago. I felt disrespected, as he tried to bring me in on his performance. I would have been fine with not speaking at all at this damn sour ass dinner party.

"Thanks," I replied, not paying him much mind and not caring to ask how he had been. I didn't wish to hear any lies or stories of the ways he had succeeded in being a fake ass punk.

"Anytime, we should catch up or something." He leaned in and whispered. He smelled amazing, the brandy on his tongue made me want to follow. And the tapered haircut and perfect fitting suit looked so damn good on him. Shaking my head, I wouldn't allow Damien to get me sidetracked.

I concentrated on the conversations around me and not reconnecting with my ex best friend that looked and smelled amazing tonight. I realized my sexual frustrations and decided to use that to my advantage. I listened intently, everyone but me was chatting. Some about important shit and others about the nasty ass food being served.

I homed in on Ryan, it was odd that he was here considering he wasn't a supporter. But it made my senses tingle because I knew there was some reason he was here. As I followed his eyes they landed on Erica. Something was up between them. I could tell from the shift in her body language. Arm no longer on Dame's back but in her lap, the sheepish look on her face, and small smile.

Jumping from my seat, I found my mother and immediately excused myself from the dinner. I had work to do. This job was feeling like a scheme, I wanted no parts of. My target had changed; it was now Erica on my radar.

Outside smoking a cigarette, I waited patiently for my uber. Considering where we were, I knew it would take some time for them to arrive, so I sat and thought of all the reasons to change my mind about Damien. I wanted so badly to ruin him, but at the same time all I wanted was to love him also. I played a good game regarding my dating life, but the older I got, the more I wanted different. The more I wanted someone to call my own, someone to love me without wanting to change me, someone to accept me, and protect me.

My heart wished it could be Damien because truthfully, for years, we were so good together. He was the thorn to my rose: the shoulder, the ear, and the beat to my heart. I remembered all the good times, and that's why that one bad time was so powerful and heavy for me. We were good together, but good wasn't good enough. He needed perfect, and that just wasn't me. It would never be me, I embraced my flaws. They made me Tru; they made me the powerhouse I was.

Lost in my thoughts, my ears began to tingle. Someone was around. It was hard to explain what I felt when adversity or conflict was present, but I felt it. Thinking quickly as I could, I felt a hand hit my shoulder. I grabbed the perp's hand and tossed them over my shoulder onto their back. What scared me was the ease, and the fact that sometimes I had no control over my strength. Have you ever felt like you had no control over yourself? Its crippling. But this was who I was now, and no matter how many times I prayed for God to take this strength away, it remained.

"Aye, Tru, chill. It's me!" he advised.

"Don't sneak up on me like that," I screamed. That was the worst thing you could do to a person with super powers. We were always on high alert and on edge. He looked wounded, but I knew only his ego was bruised and he was confused.

"How the hell you do that? I'm over two-hundred pounds!" He was still rubbing his shoulder and a small smile appeared on my face. I should've laid him on his ass years ago. Inwardly, I was pleased but I knew the questions were following.

"Adrenaline and fear bring out survival skills. Don't worry too much. Why are you out here anyway?" I asked attempting to swing the conversation.

"I saw you leave and like a magnet I followed. Now I wish I hadn't."

"I agree. Go back inside, enjoy the party, enjoy your pilgrim, and let me be." The pilgrim part slipped. I didn't mean to give any indication of bitterness. Bitterness showed that you cared, and I didn't care. I didn't care that he picked big blue eyes over my big brown eyes. I didn't care that he picked fake over something real. The more I said it the closer I was to believing that I didn't care.

"Pilgrim?" he laughed. I didn't see anything funny. She was a pilgrim and he was an Uncle Tom, but who gave a fuck about labels these days. That was their shit not mine. I needed to keep my mouth shut, I was starting to sound like a major hater.

"Is she not?" I asked. I mean, I was hoping he would surprise or wow me with some elaborate reason as to why that was inappropriate, instead he laughed again. As if I said something stand up worthy.

"I miss that about you, you always had the funniest shit to say."

I couldn't figure him out and that was disturbing me. It had been ten long summers, without him. It was too late for him to use his undeniably affective charm to ease his way back in my life.

"Why do you keep trying to take me back down memory lane?" I questioned. The facts hadn't changed. The good ole days were still the good ole days. I was the one that got away, another fact. He had me fucked up, another fact that would never change. I was a rebel, he was a peon. The same things he loved about me where the same reasons he used to crush me. Never again.

"Why can't we? Is it a crime to want to catch up with an old friend?" he asked leaning up against the pillar. His stance gave unrequested access to the massive print in his pants. I'd like to think he was turned on, but I knew he was hung like a horse. It was natural for him. It was always so easy for all the girls to flock to him. All the smiles and hair flips weren't because they cared that he had been accepted to one of the best schools in the country, they didn't care that his dream was to sail the seas in a catamaran. It was his wealth in the pockets and crotch. That's what fueled my gripes. It was always me that cared for him, the authentic him. Looking up, I brought my attention back to his soft but chiseled face. He looked like a God that I would worship with no objection. I wouldn't question his healing powers, I wouldn't question if he was real even if I couldn't see him. I would simply worship him for what he was and what he did for me when no one else was looking.

"My uber just arrived, maybe next time." I said walking fast to get away from him. The problem with a man like him was, he didn't take no for an answer. No meant defeat and that didn't sit well or roll over well.

"Where are we going?" he asked, walking quickly to catch up with me. In my head, I screamed go away, but I couldn't dismiss that after years, it was a delightful feeling to see him for once chasing me.

"Home! And alone," I fired off, what was his end game? I mean what did he really want from me and why did he all of a sudden want to reshape my perspective of him. The picture was already painted and tarnished. I didn't plan on giving him more chances to ruin me or fuck with my emotions. Emotions would supersede my intelligence. I had no time for that, although I missed the good times.

"I'm coming with. For once, I want to be normal." He said sliding in the backseat of the uber with the biggest grin on his face. Granted with me was where he belonged but tonight and right now wasn't the time.

"Normal is picking up a bitch from the bar; this isn't normal. You wait years to come around and for what Thorn?" I asked watching him buckle his seatbelt. Since taking the job, I wrestled with what I would say to him. I struggled with not letting the past affect my future, but I couldn't keep the two separate if he continued to stir up those emotions I let die. He didn't get to do that to me.

"I need a friend, Rose. Someone I can trust." He paused looking at me in my eyes. There was no hesitation or uncertainty. The voices in my head were saying be vulnerable, it'll be easier to weasel my way in and get information that could be deemed useful. But my heart was saying don't chance it.

"Fine," I grumbled as I instructed the uber to pull off. The idea of having him in my house made me edgy and tense. It was like I still wanted to impress him or show him that I had moved past the twenty-year-old me that was wounded and distraught. I wanted to show him that I didn't stay in that disappointment, but my body language showed me cowering. I was still in love.

The Truth

"Lionel, have you seen our daughter?" I asked my husband. I didn't need a hard time or for him to sit in my face and give me that look. I wanted to let Tru be her but sometimes she could do so much better. Lionel didn't understand that. To him she was perfect. To me she was too damn flighty and judgmental.

"Last I seen she stepped outside," he responded flatly.

I knew that little heffa would leave early. She never could just accept the fact that me and Darlene were friends. I don't know why she didn't like her or why she refused to be a part of our inner circles. It had so many perks that she just didn't know about. I loved Darlene, but I also kept her around in case I ever needed her.

"I swear that child stresses me out." I spoke in his ear.

"Let her be her and you be you. I dun told you that several times." He fussed as usual.

This was the shit I was talking about, he never understood where I was coming from. I was all for allowing her to be herself. But she had so much anger and rage towards the Thorns and that broke my heart. It broke my heart because she had yet to tell me why. I thought we were close but something was being hidden for me and I needed to know why. I needed to understand my own child.

"Shantay, a moment honey," Darlene requested. "Excuse us, continue to enjoy the party."

Following Darlene to the study, I was concerned with her abrupt request for my presence. We had grown up together and although one more successful than the other we were still one in the same behind closed doors. Most didn't know that, and we liked it that way.

"Girl, those damn kids of ours." She started out closing the door and grabbing two classes. Pouring the Crown in the glass, she sipped and shook her head. I didn't understand. "They left together, I knew it was a bad idea making her come."

That threw me off a little, why couldn't my daughter come around and why did two at one time close friends hanging out be an issue. "Girl, what's going on?" I asked.

Rose and Thorn were inseparable for years after she first brought him home. It was such a surprise to see him that day. It was sad that our lives had detached them to begin with. Back in the day, me and Darlene were the same way. It was only right for our kids to be the same.

"That daughter of yours, she does it every time," she rambled. "I mean Hello Damien you are set to be married to one of the most prominent families in Avia, but no he would rather chase Rose, like the puppy he is."

Now I was starting to get pissed off at Darlene and at myself. I should have seen it all along. I knew something happened with her and Thorn, but I never asked or pushed her to speak about, but it looked like Darlene was going to tell it herself.

"And what does his decision have to do with my daughter?" I asked on the verge of tying my hair back and removing my shoes. I felt a rumble coming on and it would be a lot of arranged furniture if she said something I wasn't feeling. Friend or no friend she wouldn't act as if my daughter wasn't deserving.

"Shantay, you know they can't be together. Rose is not first lady material. She's rough, too strong and a black couple will never get the respect they deserve."

"Come again Darlene," I wanted her to say what she was really trying to convey. Right now, she was pussy footing around the subject and it was raising my blood pressure. Hell, the Obama's were a black couple and they done just damn fine. My daughter wasn't some criminal and she wasn't some back-alley hoe. My Rose was just as grand if not better than Thorn.

"Damien and Rose, they can't be together. I ended that years ago, and it looks like he is going against the grain. They left together. Erica and her family are out there, and he is so close. He can't afford to make any mistakes."

"Are you saying my daughter is a mistake?" I asked removing my earrings and shoes, luckily my hair was already tied up. I was ready to pounce. I was a mother before anything else. Yeah, I was about to move this whole damn room around if she kept speaking negatively of my child. The child I raised to be strong.

"No, I love Rose, but I don't and never wanted her for my son. She's not the right one for where he is headed in life. You know that don't you?" she asked like what she said wasn't the most disrespectful shit you could ever say to the mother of the person you're downplaying.

"Bitch, let me tell you something, my damn child is perfect for whoever is lucky enough to be in her life. She's smart, she was top of her damn class. She is a lover, strong and she is her mother's damn child. Don't you ever speak of her like she is some damn peasant. I understand that politics run the nation, but love conquers the world. And I know you wouldn't understand that because you got fucked out of true love, but don't you dare put that on our children. My Child especially."

"I didn't mean to offend you, but we just have to be honest here. Rose will never add value to Damien's life. Why do you think they separated after college? He knew, he listens to me." She pleaded.

Slapping her across her face my stomach felt weak. I had no idea that Darlene felt such a way about my child. My Rose. I felt even more ill thinking of the way I pushed her to accept Darlene. I felt betrayed by my own friend. I just couldn't believe that this was happening to me.

"Shantay, please understand that I only wanna do the right thing for my family. Rose and Thorn will never be together if I have anything to do with it. I went through it and so will he. Look at me now," she said with a weak smile.

"I don't see anything but unhappiness, and what a shame it is that you want that for your own son." I felt bad for Damien as I thought about his mother planning his life and keeping him from what the world needed, love. "I'll pray for you. But you need to know that if you come for my daughter you better come hard because I will not hesitate to end you."

Slamming the door, I tapped Lionel and motioned that it was time for us to go. I couldn't be in that house a minute longer without causing a scene. How dare she say those things about my baby girl?

"What's wrong?" he asked as the valet brought our car.

"Did you know?" I asked.

"Know what?"

"About Rose and Thorn?" I whispered.

"Yeah, she didn't want to tell you because she knew how important your friendship with Darlene was. But yeah I knew when it happened."

"That bitch just told me that she wouldn't allow them to be together," I was flabbergasted as her words replayed in my head.

"It's always been like this Shantay, I love Dewayne, like a brother but ain't nobody ever coming before my baby girl." He responded sliding in the driver seat. I felt like he was throwing shade and right now wasn't a good time to be barking up my tree.

"And you think I don't feel that way?" I asked. I needed to hear it from him. I already knew I owed her an apology, but had I really been that blind to not see what was going on. I knew something wasn't right when she came home 'different'. College was like that, so I thought nothing of it. It built character and revealed things about us we didn't know. But clearly, I had been too distracted to notice or pry.

"Not intentionally but yes you get distracted by having that bitch as a friend. Now drop it; I ain't about to argue with you all night. All that damn music got my head hurting."

"I slapped her right across the face when she told me, I'd do it again for Rose."

"Do it again for you. Its clear slap in the face on who you are not just Rose."

"I hate that I didn't know and didn't say something sooner." I said shaking my head with tears in my eyes. I let her down and that weighed heavily on my heart.

"I know baby, but now you know. Let it go and call her in the morning." He responded.

I couldn't believe she would tell her father and not tell me. I was a woman and knew heartbreak. I could have, I would have been there for her through it all. I would have never spoke with Darlene again and I damn sure wouldn't have brought Damien back up. I felt like a terrible mother and I had to find a way to let her know that no one and nothing was more important than her and her happiness. I had been such a fool.

The Why

Damien Thorn was a pain in my side currently. I hated the idea of any man having more than me. Damien had looks, social skills, and he had the woman I was destined to be with. Sad thing about that is that I really didn't want to be with Erica. I just couldn't sit idly by and watch her give that man another thing that didn't belong to him. Family rules were family rules, and the worse thing I could do was go against them more than I already had.

Years ago, I decided against my parents' wishes and took up science. Secretly I had always had a thing for science. I was supposed to going down the same path as Damien, but science was more important. With that decision, I lost my running for senator and my chances at marrying Erica.

Raven's Pointe had very strict laws. Everything was literally already set in stone for the prominent families. You were expected to do as you were told so the options were limited. You followed in your father's footsteps. Failing to comply to your family's history was damn near against the law. I didn't want that; I wanted something that was full of adventure and not so black and white. It cost me almost everything until I was able to convince this town that what I did was just as important. I gained SSRP access and all the perks that came with it, but I was alone.

"Ryan, I didn't know I'd see you here," Erica said walking up to me. I hated the sight of her, despite our arrangement. Erica was spineless, but also a whore. Not the good kind of whore either, she was the type of whore that thought she wasn't.

"I was summoned," I had a simple reply for her. We weren't supposed to be communicating in public. She was Damien's property, and I'm sure, if seen together, I'd have to hear it from my father.

"Later?" she asked. Casually walking away, I wouldn't do this with her here. She was careless. She would be blackballed for going against the grain, and I wanted no parts of it.

Cheating wasn't against the law but failing to comply to your family's history was. I remained unscathed, no praise of my own. The praise belonged to my family that had the money to change the rule book. I was thankful, but it was a hard life for those with status. Commoners didn't have to live up to the same standards we did. They weren't expected to be anything other than what they wanted.

This is why I hired Tru. Damien didn't deserve this life; he wasn't a part of this life and the opportunity to see him fail kept me from sleeping. Initially, we never imagined that he would be able to make it this far, but somehow people were enjoying his bullshit promises to make Raven's Pointe an equal playing field. My colleagues and I couldn't allow that to happen, not in this lifetime.

We needed Tru to work her magic. I knew it was biased when hiring her. I knew they had history, but I also knew that he still cared for her and her for him. It wouldn't take much for her to weasel her way in and have him making a mistake. We needed a mistake. We needed the people to see that he wasn't half of what he claimed he was. It was simple. Tru gets him to open up and then we report the news, deface his character, and destroy his chances at being anything other than a commoner.

"Ryan, I'm glad you came. Let's chat," Mr. Wainwright walked up, catching me off guard. It was Mr. Wainwright who invited me to this affair. I assure you I had better shit to do but I also knew I couldn't turn down the offer.

"How's it going, sir?" I asked with a shake of the hand. It was polite even though I knew we didn't care for each other. He was disappointed and rightfully so. I was supposed to be the one to take Erica's hand. He really didn't want her with Damien, but the current senator's daughter had to marry the new senator. It was a big clusterfuck, compliments of me. However, he entrusted my help to see that Erica never made it down the aisle with him. It was the least I could do.

"Oh, cut the bullshit, Ryan. How are we looking?" he asked, cutting to the chase.

"Tru is on it, sir, no worries," I advised sipping on my cognac. This wasn't the place to get into our dealings. Apparently, Erica got her hastiness and sloppiness from her father. I personally didn't do business like this. There was a time and place for everything.

"Yeah, well Ryan they looked mighty cozy. Are you sure she's up for it?"

My tardiness to the party was a minor oversight, I hadn't seen them cozy at all. But thinking back the minute Rose left, Damien also went missing. Rose was a professional. She was a bitch, but she handled business no matter how messy it could become.

"She's fine. Tru is the best for the job. They have history. Don't sweat it." I had my apprehensions, but it wasn't enough to ask someone else. If shit got sticky, there was always a backup plan. Secrets would be revealed and before we could blink, they would be locked away like the animals they were.

"Ryan, I don't want my baby girl walking down that aisle," he said sternly. It wasn't needed. I understood, and I also knew I owed them this one favor.

"I'll see to it myself that this doesn't happen. I just need you to trust me and prepare," I had done things and knew things that really could change the game in an instant. But I didn't want to do that, I couldn't do that without exposing my hand. "Trust me," Walking off, I decided that my attendance was no longer needed. The weekend was over and before I knew it, Monday's rise would be approaching, and I'd be back in the lab attempting to get my next big break.

Heading to my car, I phoned Khalil. It was time to secure the back up. Khalil had a thing for Tru, and he would do anything to get his hands on her.

"Khalil, my friend, I need that insurance plan to kick in," I had to speak in code. I trusted Tru only a little, and I wouldn't be surprised if she had my phone bugged. I hadn't given much information to her on the reason for her services, but I knew she hated half ass shit. Knowing her, she was probably doing her own investigation into me and anyone she thought had something to do with this request.

"Done."

Everyone assumed that I disliked black people but that was far from true. Khalil and I had been friends for years, good friends. My disdain for the entire human race would be the truth. It was them that did a disservice to life. Being a white man made it easy for others to label me, but that wasn't true.

Growing up with the upper echelon required certain things. It came off racist, but it wasn't. I wanted black people to win, but they couldn't win more than I was. But Khalil and I were one in the same. We both loved science, and we both loved playing the puppet master. Our friendship was made in heaven: signed, sealed and delivered.

"Make it clean and believable." I responded. I had to cover my ass on this one. Tru wasn't one to play with. She was the best damn person for this job but also the worst person. She wouldn't hesitate to put a bullet in my head if she found out I was secretly playing her also.

"That won't be hard man, I got a thing for Tru and she plays a hard game, but I know what it takes." He replied. This was true. He had always been in love with Tru. I didn't know exactly what it was about her, but she left men falling over and sniffing behind her. Granted, she was beautiful, but her attitude wasn't anything to brag about.

"Yeah I know but the minute she thinks you are up to something fall back."

When I gave her powers, I knew she would be at my disposal. I knew she would be indebted to me, and then I got her a spot in the secret society. Anything I did had to benefit me in some way. Her powers compliments of me would be needed and also serve as plan C if shit went left.

"She's just lost Ryan, let her come around with this Thorn thing. Once she remembers who he is she will come through." He mentioned. I was glad he was so confident because I wasn't. Everything hadn't been revealed and I knew that would make what I had in works fall apart.

"Be careful, that's all I'm saying."

Pulling up to my own home, I shut the car off and made my way inside. The light in my study was on and that alarmed me. I lived alone, and I was a stickler for saving energy, so I knew someone had entered my home after I left. Tip toeing my heart was pounding and fear was on my back like a monkey.

Peeking into my study, my sister came into view. Sitting in my chair with her legs cocked up on my desk. Most brothers and sisters loved each other tremendously but me and Colleen had a hate for each other that couldn't be described.

"Hey, you piece of shit," she said. This was exactly why her and Tru got along so well, both of them where hateful bitches. Colleen more than Tru.

"Nice to see you too." I responded knocking her feet off my desk.

"Ryan, can you tell me when you became such a conniving prick?" she asked. I stared at her, wondering what her angle was. She was worked up and I had no clue as to why. I hadn't bothered her in months. Originally, I was going to ask her to take the job. I knew how upset she was with Thorn and him breaking Tru's heart. I knew it would be perfect, but I also knew that Colleen had way too many unorthodox ways. She wasn't as clean and inconspicuous as her partner.

"Sister, whatever do you mean? Have I done something to you that I am unaware of?"

"You dumb ass, you know exactly what I'm talking about!" she yelled. Her emotions got to invested. She would blow her cover before she even got started. Putting her on the job would have required damage control.

"Tru?" I asked. She came to me a few days ago asking for the job but I declined. She would kill Thorn for what he did years ago and that's not what we wanted unless it absolutely came to that. I wasn't a violent person, I didn't think it solved anything.

"Yes, you know this is a bad idea to have her so close to him. Or is that your plan? Do you plan on causing trouble for Tru?"

"Tru will only be affected if she doesn't come through with what's been asked of her. Be a good friend and make sure it doesn't come to that." I winked.

"I don't understand, we were all friends at one time. One would think that meant something to you." she challenged. This had nothing to do with friendship. This was about survival. I had no choice with my position in the secret society. When it became your time to do what was deemed right for society you did it. My hands were tied.

"This isn't about friendship, this is business."

"No this is bullshit, if it wasn't for Tru, you wouldn't be the renowned scientist you are now. She is going to get hurt. She still loves him." She screamed.

"Love can't thrive in business. There's a plan for every plan sister. Relax." I nodded.

"I hope she puts a bullet in your head, I'd do it if I could. Unfortunately, it would kill mother," she said swiping the items off my desk in a frenzy.

"See yourself out," I said heading out of the room. Being the man in charge wasn't easy but I had to do this. A lot was riding on this being successful. I would get my status back in town, Damien would brought down to size, Erica would be able to live her life on her terms and we would cancel the possibility of being the laughing stock of Avia. Colleen would get over her disdain for the situation soon or she would also be eliminated.

Second time Around

The ride to her house had me anxious. We weren't kids anymore and being alone with her may not have been the best idea. In fact, I knew it was a terrible idea. Rose and I had unfinished business, and we both knew it and fought it at the same time. Who would be the first to address this business still remained a mystery. It would most likely be me, and I was fine with that. Her composed manner was a front and only I knew that. She got angry and irritated when her hand was being forced. So, the smiles, laughs, and easy conversation flowing between us as we drove was bogus. But I still pressed on as if I was none the wiser of her discomfort.

"Dame listen, I still don't know why you decided to force this but let me tell you right now," she paused before speaking. It was kind of her to search for the right words, "I need Thorn, not that brat, tight suit wearing, prick that hurt me to the core years ago. If you can't be that, let me pay for your uber home."

Little did she know I wanted to be Thorn, if only for one night. I wanted to chill, leave my shoes in the floor, drink malt liquor and listen to some good music, "You read my mind" I said unbuttoning my suit jacket and loosening my tie.

"Are you sure?" she asked me shocked that I was excited to be back to my college days.

"Let's go!" I said offering my hand as we pulled up to her building. It was nice, surprisingly fancy for my Rose. Not that she didn't enjoy the finer things, she was just grungy, simple, and eccentric. She listened to Erykah Badu, she loved Sade playing while incense burned, and she even knew the moon schedules. Those were her things and as much as I hated them back then I could appreciate the simplicity she loved now. Erica always needed shit to be perfect and poised. That took away from the beauty of things. She never allowed things to fall apart so they could come back together. It was so mundane, and as I followed Tru into her apartment, I realized what I had been missing, my sanity.

Her apartment was brick on the inside, although it was a penthouse. The elegant throwback couches fit her personality, the messy mail was thrown on the end table, and I could smell her favorite incense lingering in the air. I was amazed that she still burned the celestial scent. Damn, the memories came flooding back.

"No shoes," she warned. Removing my shoes and coming in further, I took a seat on the couch and watched her kick off her strappy heels, unzip her dress, and let it drop to the floor. She pranced around in her matching black set of underwear. I tried to peel my eyes away, but it wasn't easy. It felt like college again. Her body was so damn toned, her smooth skin was endless, and my God she looked like a Hershey's kiss waiting to be unwrapped.

"Let me change, and I'll throw on Cooley High. You still like that movie, right?" She asked, jarring me out of my helpless thoughts.

I cleared my throat and swallowed my desires, "Yeah, I haven't seen it in years."

"Cool, give me a sec." Her voice was distant, and I assumed that her room was the furthest back. I was tempted to take my chances and sneak back and take a peek, but I wasn't a creep and I knew it would open a door I wouldn't be able to close this go around, so I sat. The longer she took, the more uncomfortable I was. I was shifting, rearranging, and making sure I didn't come off as a total fool.

Coming back out, she was in a crop top, spandex shorts that hugged her ass perfectly, her hair in a pineapple, and glasses on. She was still comfortable around me and that made me loosen up. I had no reason to be nervous around her. This was me and her. I knew everything about her. I knew her likes and dislikes, I knew the shit that she felt passionately about, and I even knew the shit she thought no one knew.

"You want a wine cooler?" she asked sitting on the floor, stretching. I heard her, but I couldn't take my eyes off the scars on her back. I wanted to touch them, I wanted to ask what happened, and I wondered if this happened when after I left her wondering if she was enough for me. "Stop staring at my scars. Shit happens."

"What happened?" I asked. Not asking was impossible, I had so many questions. They were small and circular, like she had a bad experience with acupuncture, but they were in a row and perfect.

"It's nothing. Drink?"

"Yeah, what kind you got in there?" I asked. I would leave it alone for the moment. I planned on seeing her more. I wanted to make things right before I regretted them more than I already had. As she went to the kitchen, the memory of the evening that we ended our seamless friendship came to the forefront of my mind.

Meet me at town hall, Rose

I knew she was in class and would chew me up if I called her phone and distracted her. My Rose had a slight case of ADD. She couldn't focus on multiple things at once. So texting was best as I gathered my thoughts and figured out how I would break the news to her.

K.

Sliding my phone in my pocket, I felt a tap on my shoulder. Turning to look, it was Rose, "I thought you had class," I asked. I knew her schedule like the back of my hand. We planned all our outings around our school schedule; it was imperative that we both succeeded. Especially, because we were two of the five African American students to attend such a prestigious school.

"I did, but when Thorn needs his Rose, she appears, now what's up?" she asked hugging my waist. She was shorter than me. I was a giant while she was a shrimp compared to me.

108

"Let's sit on the bench," I directed nervously.

"Cool, everything ok?" she asked touching my forehead. I could see the concern appear on her face, and pain was soon to appear on mine once I said what needed to be said. Not wanted but needed, that had to be understood. I knew her well enough to know her face would soon be littered with disappointment and then hate. I was dreading the conversation before it even began. It wasn't supposed to be this way between us. We were friends, but over the years, we couldn't deny that something else had grown. I had never been in this position before. Women were easy for me, but Rose she was different. She made me work for her respect and that was why it had to end.

"You know you will always be the Rose to my Thorn, right?"

"Of course, what's a rose with no thorns?" she asked, and she was right. I was nothing without her. She was the pain in my ass, the light of my path, she was the fiction to my facts, and the voice to my reason.

"Nothing, absolutely nothing." I was stalling scared as fuck to tell her that this wasn't going to work. Where I was going, she couldn't go. I felt like a soldier in the army deploying for the first time. I was completely unsure of my return.

"Damien, you are stalling just tell me. Are you transferring?" she asked cluelessly.

"Tru, please forgive me for what I'm about to do." Looking in her eyes made it harder to say what I had to say. So sweet, patient, and so damn kind.

"Just say it Dame, I don't need you pacifying me," she said close to a scream. She could feel the tension; the heat was rising on this dreary winter day. I was starting to sweat and play out all the ways this could and would go.

"After graduation, I... I can't do this with you. Us can't be a thing." I said it convincing myself more than her.

"I don't understand. Why can't we be friends?" she asked, knowing that we had moved past friends. I understood the line of questioning; we both pretended a platonic friendship was what we had. But we were only fooling ourselves. The late-night study sessions, the hanging with each other twenty-four seven, the secret glances at each other when we kicked it. We knew, we just never addressed it.

"Tru, you are too ethnic for what I have going on right now. I love it but it's not good for my image. I've decided to follow in my father's footsteps." I breathed.

"Your mother is black, so I still don't understand what you are trying to say."

"Yeah, but my mother isn't you. I've always loved that about you but now right now, it can't be that way." I confessed.

"Wow, this is bullshit and you fucking know it. I thought... I thought we had the sweetest taboo, the highest vibration, so that was all a lie?" she quizzed quickly. Her questions were coming so quick I couldn't possibly answer them. Not to mention none of my answers would make sense because this was so fucked up to do.

We had a drunk night where sober thoughts came out and we said some shit that we couldn't take back. It wasn't a lie. She was it, she was the one, but it wouldn't work. She wouldn't adapt, she wouldn't hold her tongue, and she would have me caught up in a bunch of mess. She was for Thorn, not for Damien Maliek Thorn future president of Avia. My mother wasn't having it. She loved Trulicity, but not as my wife.

It was just two weeks ago over Christmas dinner that she denied my request to ask for Tru's hand in marriage. The conversation didn't sit well with me that day, but by the end, she had me convinced that this was the right and only way I could have success.

"That shit is and will always be true, but right now I have to focus on my future."

"Wow, so I'm not a part of your future?"

"I have to do what's best for me and where I want to go in life. I love you Rose, I mean I really do. I want this as much as you do but we have to be honest. We need to do what's best for us both."

Why do you think you always know what's best for me? This isn't best for me this is best for you." she asked.

"This hurts me just as it hurts you. I'm left with no options. Please say you understand that I've got to leave this here."

"Yeah, I understand. You do what you need to do, and I truly wish you luck," she said with tears in her eyes. That disappointment was there and overshadowing any other emotions she was feeling. I fucked up and felt my heart sinking to my feet as she cried and clutched her stomach.

Scooting over to hug her, she moved and jumped up before I could touch her. I would forever remember the look she had in her eyes. It was one of anger and sympathy.

"I'm sorry," I muttered. I meant that. The position we were in was uncomfortable and completely ignorant. It almost made no sense, Rose came from a good home, we were in the same college, and we both had drive and dreams, but without saying it, she was too black for me. She was too flawed to be on my arm as I climbed my way to the top.

"Yeah me too, I'm sorry that my black intimidates you, I'm sorry that you for whatever reason think that I can't contribute to your success, and I'm really sorry that you will never know a love like mine. I love you, Thorn. Always have. Even when I knew it would never be more than what it was. And now all you have to say is sorry for breaking my heart and ultimately telling me that I'm too black. You sound just like them and I feel bad for you. I wish you luck and success." Caressing my face, she left me sitting right there on that bench with my heart in her bookbag. I watched her walk away until I couldn't see her anymore. My heart said move, chase after her but my feet and ass were planted. I couldn't move, it was best that I let her go her way I went mine.

We never spoke again until now. Watching her walk away that day made the temperature drop. My blood stopped flowing my heart stopped pumping. I was dead. That started the transformation into who I was today: prudish, lame, and someone not in control of my own brain or destiny. I envied her, I envied her strength. I always prayed our paths would cross again. There were several times, I grabbed my phone to hit her up and check on her, but I didn't. And here she was still strong, still honest, and still Rose. I didn't anticipate it being this way, you know with so many unanswered questions and unspoken words. I had so much I wanted to say.

"Here, I know it's not that fancy shit you used to, but it'll do the trick" she giggled. Still untroubled, still soft, and still playing like she was happy that I was in her space. She hadn't changed a bit.

"I'm sick of fancy shit. Do you know how much I wish I could just wake up and stay in the house, watch movies, and eat junk food? I miss that shit."

"Well let's do it tonight!" her offer was enticing, but if I got to comfortable, I would never want to leave. Her aura was like quicksand, it sucked you in with little effort. I'd never make it home and I'd never follow through with my plans.

"I can't stay long, but I appreciate you trying to help a brotha out."

"So, let's cut the crap, why are you here?" She sat back down at my feet and rested on my knee, waiting for an answer, "I mean are you here on some let me make up for what I did? Because if so, I don't need it. You were right"

"No I wasn't, and you know it. What I did was fucked up," I admitted. It weighed on me. For years, I didn't have to address it. We hadn't been around or seen each other. We were in different circles, and it helped me not think about what we shared. But since seeing her again, it was back. The guilt was sitting on my shoulders, like heavy boulders.

"It was, but I decided not to let the hurt define or stop my journey. I understood," She said sipping her wine cooler, her eyes didn't read that she was over it. "You were in a broken place, no harm in that. I needed to face the hard truth in order to get to where I am now. I confused your attention for love."

"I never deserved you. I didn't then, and I don't know. I'm just going to go," standing to leave she stopped me.

Since Los brought her up, she had been on my mind constantly. I could be brushing my teeth and visions of her hugging me from behind could be seen, getting my haircut reminded me of her training my waves all those years ago. The patience she had with me, when I started to get a whiff of myself, I would be late to study sessions too busy chatting with females, and she would be right there waiting. My choices allowed me to have the life I wanted but removed the opportunity to have love. She would continually be on my mind, and that's where she had to stay. I couldn't bring her in this mess that I had yet to completely sort out. I was set to marry Erica. I was set to win this election by a landslide and she still didn't fit.

Unravel Me

Watching him stand to walk out of my life again couldn't happen. I was willing to be friends again; I was willing to be anything that he needed me to be as long as it was with him. Damien was the love of my life, and you never get over that one person. I reviled that it had to come to this, I was trying to avoid it to the best of my abilities. But that damn mother of mine insisted that I be there, and now we were stuck toying with the idea of addressing the bullshit that happened or not addressing it.

As I got the drinks, I watched his face contort into one of darkness, he was re-living the day he made the decision to let what we had fall by the wayside. I remembered to, but I tried not to think about it. I had to withdraw myself from those thoughts. I refused to allow what he did to mold me into someone that couldn't trust anyone. He didn't deserve to rearrange me or mold me into someone with trust issues. He had his opinion of me and I had mine.

I wanted ghetto love and he wanted contract love. It wasn't for me. But I wouldn't dare judge or condemn him for it. He was raised up in the shit, it was inevitable. I assumed he would be stronger than that, but I also knew he wanted to please his parents, well Darlene's fake ass. I never stood a chance, and it was my fault that I thought I could change the dynamic of what he was used to. I set myself up for failure and disappointment.

"Why are you leaving?" I asked curious as to why he all of a sudden cared about the past. It was behind me; I changed my story. I re- wrote my future. God intervened by removing negativity. His mother would have never allowed us to live a life of peace. He would always be attempting dummy missions to prove himself worthy to her. I couldn't compete with that nor would I be able to sit back and watch. That's what he meant by me being to ethnic. I wouldn't allow his mother to take advantage of his love for her.

"I made a mistake by even coming. I'm sure Erica is looking for me,"

"Fuck her, if she was looking for you, she would have called by now," I said sick of hearing about Erica. I was disgusted with his choice. It was something about her that gave me a bad feeling. I couldn't put my finger on it, but something wasn't right.

"I left my phone on purpose," he admitted with a small smile.

"Sit back down, let's watch this movie, and after that, if you want to leave, you can. Deal?"

He chewed on the inside of his lip when he was nervous or in deep thought. I didn't understand what was so wrong with watching a movie. We had never crossed the line of intimacy before, and I wouldn't tonight. I didn't care for Erica and I was human, but I wasn't desperate. Damien made it clear years ago that we couldn't cross that line, and I refused to give him access to a part of me he hadn't earned access to. I wouldn't play the game of love again; it wouldn't make a fool out of me. I couldn't afford to give my heart to any of these niggas. Not now, not while I was in my prime.

"Why are you letting me stay?" he asked.

"Why not? You said you wanted to be normal for one night, and I wanted to be a part of that. We ended shit terribly, but we had a friendship that should have been unbreakable." I answered. I was crossing into dark territory, but fuck it, "I hated you for so long. It took time, but eventually, I began to understand and then I began to feel sorry for you. It's a hard life trying to live up to others' standards, trust me I know," He may have never seen it, but once the realization hit that I loved and wanted more with him, I changed. I tried hard, to be a little less loud, I tried hard to tame my hair sometimes, wear less black and in the end, it still turned out to not be enough to win him over or keep him from crossing over.

"How do you know about that? The Tru I know didn't follow or care about standards," he was right, but he failed to pay attention. I knew the minute things changed with us. He stopped coming around and he stopped reaching out to me. He no longer needed my help studying. A woman's intuition was never wrong. I felt it, without words.

"Trust me I know. For a minute, I allowed you to change me. You didn't notice but it happened. When you came back from Christmas vacation, I could hear it in your voice, see it in your tired, confused eyes. I knew way before you mentioned it."

"Why didn't you say something?" he asked like it was something that was easy to say or bring up. Thinking back, it was mostly all about him. Me always waiting on him, me always hanging on to him. It wasn't him, he wasn't the one that made us so strong and special. It was my dedication that carried us so far.

"Remember when you came to my dorm, we were supposed to hang out and when you walked in you asked what happened to my hair?"

"Yeah barely, you loved your afro, but this day it looked like you picked it out or something."

"Earlier that day, I went to the shop on Trainer and West, I let them straighten my hair. I thought you would love it, but you didn't. I tried so hard to be what you wanted but your mind was made up." I admitted. He joked the entire night that someone fucked up my hair, and that I had better wash it out before class. I was hurt, so hurt by his words. So offended that I barely said a word the rest of the night. What he thought was me being upset with the jokes, was me being upset that my attempt was overlooked and turned into a joke.

"Damn, I'm an idiot" he said shaking his head.

"After you finally grew balls to tell me what was going on, I went back to my dorm and I cried. I cried like I was watching Cochise die in Cooley High, I cried like when Baby finally got to dance with Johnny in front her parents, I cried like when Cleo dies in Set it Off."

"I can't say sorry enough," he mumbled.

"I don't want your apologies. I want you to make sure it was worth it," I wanted success for Damien. We all deserved success. We all deserved to win. I wouldn't hold that shit from ten years ago against him. Now that my life had turned and came full circle, I was happy that he let me go. I would have never been able to live the life I wanted with him. The public scrutiny and eyes on us constantly would have stressed me to the point of divorce, and that wasn't an option. I loved my life, I loved being my own person, I loved making my own rules. If I didn't want to shave, I didn't have to. If I didn't want to cook, I didn't have to. If I didn't want to be bothered, I didn't have to. I was free to go and come as I pleased. I answered to no one. I was able to work a job that fulfilled me and allowed me to live in my passion. I was able to be a bad ass and not have that minimized by a man. I was a phenomenal woman, and no one could take that from me.

"You will make someone a happy man one day,"

"Don't waste your time with sweet nothings" I said turning to play the movie. It was getting a smidgen too serious and that wasn't the plan. I had no intentions of bringing up the dead, but it felt good to finally address the shit that kept me from sleeping, eating, and loving for years.

"If I told you I wish I could do it over, would you believe me?" he asked. I pondered on the question, because I believe that everything happened for a reason. Some shit was either meant to make or break you and some shit was just fucked up, "Yes, I believe that regrets are a part of life. We live, and we learn, Dame"

"Good. I want to show you something." I watched him remove his jacket and his shirt, biceps bulging as his smooth skin came into display and then the most beautiful mural displayed on his rib. It was me, tangled in roses and vines.

"When?" I asked covering my mouth. I was speechless and confused.

"Not important," he replied.

Like hell it wasn't. I needed to know when he I crossed his mind and forced him to defy his parents and mark up his body. "I was a fool to think that letting you go was the best for me. And I mean that in any facet, there were so many times I wished I could hear your voice and see your face. I got tired of picking up the phone and tossing it. So, I did something that would remind me every time of what you meant to me. It was like a 'what would rose do' mural,"

"Did it help?" I asked. I hoped it wasn't in vain. He would never be able to get rid of that, but who would want to? It was beautiful, detailed and it was me.

"Hell yeahh, it did, I went into a lot of meetings feeling like shit and would remember you saying, 'Dame, don't think about the thorn, think about the rose attached,' Id laugh, go in and kill it."

"It's beautiful," I couldn't say much else than that. I felt my emotions attempting to bubble over. I was sad because even though he thought I wouldn't be good for his career, it was me that assisted him in some way and then again amazement settled in, I was amazed that he recognized what I meant to him. This was going to get difficult and messy. Playing the movie, I grabbed my blanket and got comfortable. Cheers to healing.

When Midnight Strikes

The hairs on the back of neck started to stand at attention, the ache in my head let me know something was wrong. Damien was asleep on my small couch; he was comfortable and free. I hoped whatever it was going on would end. I couldn't afford to blow my cover or have Dame asking more questions than I had answers to.

Calm down I coached myself. I could hear the indistinct yelling through my door, but as the yelling continued I felt the strength rush to my legs, my arms, and my breathing increase. It was happening.

Grabbing my jacket and slipping on my boots, I put my hood on hoping to conceal my identity. I loved saving those in need, but I hated being put in compromising situations. What I did to save others could bring harm to me or damage my credibility within my field.

Slipping out the balcony door, I looked back and could see the rise and fall of his chest and decided it was good to move. Those cheap ass drinks always did the trick. He was knocked out. Hopefully, I could do my good deed of the day, calm down, and make it back before he woke up.

Following the screams and the glass crashing, my veins started to bulge. The transformation was getting stronger. For years, I was scared but now it was a part of my life. "Cedric, stop," I heard as I climbed up the balcony. It pissed me off when men thought they could hit on women and push their weight around. Fear didn't belong to live in women. We shouldn't be afraid to love or be afraid to stand up for ourselves. That wasn't love.

Getting closer to the altercation, my ears started to ring. That was the telltale sign that the transformation was complete and that I was close. Breathing in and out, I kicked in the door. I was always one for a dramatic entrance. I wasn't worried about anyone coming. They should have intervened before now. I had the third floor to myself but beneath me there were at least seven apartments all occupied. I shook my head at the mess. Glass was scattered, holes in the wall and couches slashed.

"Give me the money and I go away. I told you, I need my fix."

I groaned at the desperation and weakness dripping from his, well Cedric's voice. Rounding the corner, I saw him standing over her with a knife in hand. She was crouching down, black eye forming and scratches all over her body. Cracking my neck, I again prayed that she wasn't one of those women that wanted to save their abuser. I've had several of them before. Save the women and get disrespected by them in the same breath. That was a thorn to the rose of saving people. You never knew who would appreciate the power you possessed or the help you provided. Some thanked me and kissed my hands and others called me freak, weirdo and threatened to call the police. It blew my mind how easy it was for those that were being abused to turn and protect the same ones that hurt them. Another thorn was understanding that if they weren't ready you couldn't make them be ready.

"Ahhhh!" she screamed finally noticing me.

"Cedric, we can do this the easy way or the hard way!" I said looking at him in his dead and dangerous eyes. He was dope sick and although I never experienced being with someone that was a user I understand co-dependency. Another thorn. I felt too much, I cared too much and ultimately wanted to save everyone.

"Fuck you, bitch," he screamed turning to me with the knife. I watched her scurry away and come behind me.

"So, the hard way is your choice I see." Cracking my knuckles, I got closer. Once the powers took over, I also had skin as tough as Teflon. I was a true mutant. I had so many powers and hidden things I could do some of them surprised me.

"I just need money," he shook violently.

I just kept my eyes trained on him and the knife as I listened to him make excuses for his poor choices and disrespect.

"She made me hit her, I didn't want to. I just need money, Tricia," he scratched. Looking around again, I wanted to make sure I didn't miss anything. The living room was trashed, and the kitchen was where I found them. I needed to make sure no kids were around. I hated to do this shit in front of kids.

"I understand, I really do, but you mean to tell me you grew those arms and can't control them?" I asked coming closer, the moment I saw weakness in his eyes, I kicked him in the chest and watched him fly into the kitchen table. Grabbing the knife that flew from his hands, I stood over him and now he was at the mercy of me and Tricia, "Oh no Cedric, you looked dazed." I poked.

"What are you?" he asked. That was always the question I got it never surprised me. He would have a bruise in the morning, he would tell the police that some crazy woman came in and did these things to him and they wouldn't believe him. The roles would be reversed. I'm sure Tricia had told several people of his abuse. I could tell by looking at the old wounds healing. No one had her back or believed her, and I'd be sure he dealt with the same.

Grabbing the arm he hit her with, I snapped it in half. "Ahhhhhhh!" he screamed in pain. Oh, the sweet sound of doing to others, was so melodic.

"You see, now you really have no control of your arm. If I find out you've been here fucking with her, next time I'll take it with me. Do I make myself clear?" I asked dropping the arm. He screamed again. Standing to my feet, I wasn't satisfied, but I needed to wrap this up. With my boot on his arm, I asked again, "Are we clear?"

I'm sure he was delirious from the excruciating pain he was in, but I still needed an answer, or he would miraculously fall down four flights. Stepping harder, I waited for an answer as he came in and out of consciousness. "Tricia, you good?"

"Who are you?" she asked.

Blowing an exasperated breath, I answered, "it depends on the time of day, at night I go by the Grim Reaper, the choice is up to Cedric." Who I was, wasn't important. What was important was that she was safe and would be able to heal and do better. She wouldn't have to worry about Cedric anymore.

"Thank you!"

"Don't mention it, call the police," I instructed. My job here was done it was time for Raven's Point PD to do its job, and if they didn't, I'd be back, bringing more pain and it wouldn't pretty. I hated a mufucka that didn't take heed to lessons or my directions.

Headed out the door, a small voice stopped me, "Are you a super-hero?" Standing there was a sleepy boy in wolverine pajama's holding a teddy bear and rubbing his eyes.

"Yep, and so are you! Protect your momma, ok?" I had a soft spot for kids. The sheer innocence they often possessed made me smile. Childhood was taken so lightly. We were always in a rush to grow up and get in the real world. Often oblivious to the evils, the immorality, and the corruption lurking. Life swallowed you up spit you out and then sometimes it didn't. Life would keep you captive. It was important to be a child for as long as you could. 'Don't rush it,' my momma use to say. And what did I do, rush it. I rushed the hell out of it. I rushed off to college ready to declare my independence. I rushed my virginity, I rushed to bills, debt, and heartache. And let's not forget disappointment.

At the window, I crouched on the balcony and jumped to my own balcony. I couldn't be seen on the elevator; it would raise to many questions. Letting the breeze calm me down, I looked out at the land before me. The lights twinkled, the air was still and calming. Sighing, I thanked God, for keeping me safe and sane. I prayed for the ability to keep my people safe. I prayed for understanding of what I was feeling. My heart was ready for love, but not if it wasn't with him, the him on my couch, the him that wasn't mine to have. The him that didn't deserve me. The him that if he wanted a second chance could have one.

Lord, I don't know what I'm doing, I admitted. I could admit when I was lost, it was the only way clarity could follow. I needed clarity, I needed a sign.

He Knows

"I knew it," I whispered. She wasn't as inconspicuous as she thought she was. I followed her when she snuck out. I watched her kick that door down, I watched her jump from balcony to balcony with ease. I still felt the pain in my shoulder from the slam to the ground. It was all starting to make sense.

"Knew what?" she asked, she looked like a deer caught in headlights. But I refused to let her shut me out. I know what I witnessed and what I witnessed was not something you could turn your cheek too.

"You have powers," I wanted so bad for her to just admit it. But the look in her eyes, well the indifference in her eyes let me know it wouldn't be so easy. She didn't trust me.

"Get out!" she groaned. I read the look wrong, she was still coming down. But my feet were cemented to the ground, I couldn't move. I didn't want to move. I wanted to see it for myself. I wanted to hear it for myself.

"NO!" I said standing my ground. I watched as she came closer, I closed my eyes preparing for the wrath that was sure to come, but as she got closer, I could hear her gasped. Slowly opening my eyes, I looked down at my hands. The thorns had appeared. Rose wasn't as different as she thought. I to had powers.

"How?" she asked grabbing my hands. Turning them from one side to the other she examined the thorns, "This isn't possible" she muttered.

"Trust me, I didn't ask for this" I was ebullient with someone finally knowing the real me. I've had to hide and be careful. I've had to lie and cancel engagements all in the name of science. I didn't even ask for this shit. It wasn't in the cards, and it damn sure wasn't something I grew up believing was possible. I raised on concrete and factual shit. My parents did allow the idea of make-believe shit or fairy tales. It either was or it wasn't.

"Who did this to you?" she asked.

"One-night Ryan came to me and asked if I wanted to be a part of some research for his final grade. I fucked with Ryan all though he was always on some fuck shit," Ryan was your typical white guy, from power, long money and even longer family history. He pretended to like those different from him, but we were all pawns. It had been that way for years. His great grandfather was said to be a mad scientist and the reason Raven's Pointe was built the way it was. The whole idea of us being a separate state was his people's idea. Ryan used others to advance science and ultimately created a league of super individuals that were ready to set it off for the good of the people. "I agreed, and now my physique changes and thorns appear in times of distress."

She was in awe, or was it confusion? I couldn't tell, her face was unreadable. She looked confused, but the wheels also seemed to be turning in her head.

"Now I need to tell you something?" She closed the balcony door and making sure all the windows and doors were locked. Now she was starting to worry me, she was acting as if someone was watching, "Ryan hired me, well tried to hire me to find dirt on you. I need to know why."

I could think of several reasons why Ryan would want something on me. But what alarmed me was that he entrusted her to do it knowing we were friends, good friends. We hung in the same circle in college, and he knows our families are close.

"Ryan wants Erica. He was always supposed to have Erica. It was his grandparents wishes."

"This is about flat ass Erica! Does she know? Is that why you marryin' her?" she fired off. Pacing the floor, she was cute as fuck upset. I remembered that too.

"Partially about Erica, Ryan doesn't want me in power, because he probably thinks I will shut his study down. But that's the furthest from my mind," I wouldn't shut Ryan down, but I would force him to do the right thing and that was help the people. People were sick and in need of cures. His idea could save the world. But that didn't interest him.

She was pacing the floor, visibly shaken by what she was seeing and me I was struggling to not go on a rampage. I couldn't control my powers like I wished. They didn't happen as often as they used to. I also wasn't clear on my triggers. Other than danger, and stress I had no clue what set me off. All I know is that it took hours to come back to my normal self.

"Dame, you can't tell anyone else," she said coming closer. Touching my arm, the thorns disappeared, and my heart slowed down. Collapsing onto the couch, she rushed to get me water. I was in shock; she was the antidote. She was the restorative power.

"Rose, you are the antidote." I whispered. My powers drained me, I couldn't function after the transformation ended. Normally due to the length of the moment. Because I had no clue how to handle my moments I typically stayed in them more than I felt was normal.

"What?" she asked.

"You are the antidote, normally it takes me hours to revert back. I know it seems strange but not really," I was so happy that this was something else we shared. Touching the side of her face, "When?"

"Thorn, no we can't do this right now. I need to get my thoughts together." Watching her move around frantically, I couldn't figure out what she was looking for. "This changes shit," she muttered.

"No, it doesn't," I confessed. This was the sign I was looking for; she was still the one for me. Knowing that I wasn't alone would make it easier for me to cancel shit with Erica.

Tossing a manila folder in my lap, I looked at the contents. It was profile on me from Ryan, nothing in the folder mentioned my super powers. "You can't marry Erica, not with this. Plus, she payin' someone large amounts of money. I need time to track it down."

"Fuck Erica," I wasn't concerned with what she did with her money.

"No, we have to cause a diversion Thorn." She was correct, but I hadn't found a way to get out of it and reach my dreams. It was a one-way street. Either I married Erica and became senator, or I didn't and be back at square one, "Well, let's figure something out." I mentioned. I needed her help. I needed her to pretend to do her job but help me in the process.

"How can I help you when he has dirt on me also?"

She was right, but we would have to put our heads together to take Ryan down. We would have to make him look worse than what he wanted me to look.

"We need to expose Ryan," I offered. It was the only way we would be able to stay free. The minute people found out about our powers and identities we would be locked away like animals. I didn't want that for Rose, and I didn't want that for myself. I loved her enough to protect her like she protected everyone else. I needed time to grow and that growth had taken place., "Think about it, and let me know."

I stood to leave but before I could touch the door handle, she rushed me. It was the sweetest kiss. I couldn't lie, it was long overdue, but we had to play it safe and be careful.

"I'll see you soon. We can do this," I spoke leaving. I had to man up and shield Rose like I should've done all those years ago. I felt good, I felt like I had someone on my side. I had to take some time out and handle what was brewing between me and Rose. Once Ryan was handled, I would be handling me and Rose. A new horizon would soon be coming into view.

Restless Thoughts

My mind was so restless since I was left to deal with my thoughts alone. Thorn leaving was a bad idea and I was feeling terrible about. I should have made him stay and tell me what happened and when he got fucked by Ryan. I understood why he left, the revelations of our past were probably too much to bear, but damn I had questions. I needed to know if he too felt like this was a gift and a curse. I had been laying her for hours tossing and turning with no answers to the questions I had. It was giving me anxiety like no other. Tossing the covers off I decided to see if I could get some work accomplished. I needed to track down this money and figure out a plan to get us on top and from under Ryan's claws.

Grabbing my phone, I noticed a message from my mother. I was hesitant to open it and read it. I knew she was most likely upset with my abrupt departure. I planned to explain everything to her soon. I owed her an explanation for a lot of shit that had been swept under the rug. But as I opened the message and my heart sank to my feet.

Mommy: Rose, your mother is sorry. I had no idea that Darlene had sabotaged you and Thorn. I'm pissed. I wish I could say I was hurt by you not telling me, but I also understand that my head was so far up Darlene's ass that I probably made you feel that I wouldn't be as accepting. I'll carry that. No one on this earth is more important than you and your happiness. Love you, and call me later.

I didn't know how she found out, I knew my father didn't tell her. He was the best at keeping secrets. Truly I didn't care how she found out. I was just glad I didn't have to be the one that broke her heart and busted her bubble about Darlene. It was true when they said that times changed the older you got. It was no longer my mother shielding me from people and situations of the world. It was me protecting her. I wanted my mother happy, she deserved happiness.

I smiled at her apology, but I had to let her know that there was no guilt to carry. I was an adult and I never felt as though my mother put anyone before me. I valued my friendships and I know I got that from my mother. I held my tongue because of my love for her and because I carried hope that everything done in the dark soon came to light. I dug up shit and exposed people for a living. Sometimes I got a thrill from seeing the look in people's eye when they realized those that held so high where so filthy. I would never do that to my own mother, not for all the money in the world.

"Love you, Mommy," I spoke into the air. I used to do this in college all the time. We had that type of connection. I knew somehow someway she would hear that single whisper from me and it would ease her mind and lonely heart.

Stepping into my home office, I powered up my computer and gathered all the things I had on Thorn. All that was attached to him would be attached to her. I needed to track this money down, I was sure this would tell its own story.

Staring at the photos, I started to see a pattern. Her father who was stepping down as the senator didn't look happy about his daughter's engagement. In each picture his smug face told a story of disgust. I could bet that this was the reason we got involved.

Grabbing my phone, I called Colleen, I knew it was late, but I needed her to break down the dynamics of the Wainwrights and their connection to her family. Damien mentioned that being why Ryan didn't fuck with him anymore.

"Hey girl, everything ok?" she asked answering the phone. I felt terrible because it was nighttime, but this was so important it couldn't wait.

"Everything's fine, I've got some questions only you can answer."

"Let me get to my office, one sec." Hearing her shuffle and move about got me to looking a little closer at her financial records. She owned a few properties some I had never heard of but would look into those also. *"Ok, what's up?"* she asked.

"I need to know about Erica, well the Wainwrights, and Ryan. I need to know why Ryan is so invested in this." I felt a tug at my heart for asking. She owed Ryan loyalty whether I liked it or not. I was always putting her in bad situations.

"Ryan was supposed to be senator and marry the senator's daughter. It's how they keep a hand in politics. Senator Wainwright knows that won't be the case with Damien."

"Ok, so get rid of Damien then who becomes senator?" It didn't make much sense if they cancelled his run for senator the process would start all over.

"Erica," she yawned.

"How? Women can't be senators!"

"Oh, you have it wrong, they can't run for senator, but if your husband passes or is demoted, it automatically passes to you. Avia changed that years ago. Remember Madam Bennet?"

"Shit!" It was all making sense. They didn't want to expose Damien they wanted a reason or probable cause to execute him. "Why didn't you tell me this at first?" I asked, shocked by the revelation of what was being said.

"Damien doesn't deserve you or the senator position. It just dawned on me what they were doing," she responded. I didn't know if I could believe her, she hated Damien, she was Ryan's sister. But this didn't benefit her any in way. Not that I knew of.

"Thanks, see you at work." I disconnected quickly. I felt some type of way about her withholding information. We were a team, meaning if I needed any information she was supposed to give it freely. I blamed Ryan he knew this was a conflict of interest for not only me but for his own sister. Their families were connected although Colleen didn't fuck with them.

Grabbing for my bottle of water, I noticed a check on my desk. Picking it up, I felt like the luckiest bitch in the world. Staring at the check a big grin formed on my face. The account matched the bank account Erica was sending money to.

"Yahtzee!" I yelled and danced. Erica was paying Ryan for this job. I knew something was up with the strong faced bitch. And honestly if my thoughts were correct it wasn't really Erica, it was her father that wanted to get rid of Damien and he used her account because his is closely tracked.

"I got you, bitch." I wanted to call Damien until I realized that we didn't even exchange numbers. That was dumb, but I was sure I'd see him soon. Real soon.

The Next Day

I sat in my office spinning in my chair as if I didn't have anything better to do until a knock on my door startled me. "Come in," I advised. With my back still to the door I could smell her perfume, it was the same shit Darlene gave me one year for Christmas. *What a bitch* I thought.

"The door." I motioned. I wouldn't have any conversations with her without my door closed. It was an easy way to cover myself. Once the door closed the recorder started for my own safety.

"Can I offer you something to drink?" I asked Erica as she sat down with her panty hose covered legs. She still looked old and shriveled but her outfit was a little less formal. I could appreciate a girl coming down to the slums and being normal.

"Tea, please"

"Ok it's over there on the bar," She looked shocked that she, Erica Wainwright would have to prepare her own beverage. I laughed, "Just kidding,"

Preparing her tea, I felt her eyes on me. She was studying me. Attempting to figure out what I had that she didn't. Only problem with that is that what I possessed that trumped her, couldn't be seen. It wasn't my looks; white women had always been more desirable in the eyes of society. It was the peace, it was the inner beauty, it was the history we black women possessed.

"How can I help you?" I asked.

"I totally only came down here because I think we need to get to know each other. You obviously know more about me than I do you, let's make it even." She said with so much zest.

"No thank you!"

"I don't understand your disdain for me. Me and Damien are set to be married in a few weeks and it's important that I make his friends understand that they will be my friends." She explained

I rolled my eyes, because I made it clear that we weren't friends days ago. When she attempted to throw her weight around. "It's important that you understand that me and Damien aren't friends. We went to college together. Simple."

I wanted to tell her how I had no desire to be her friend because soon I'd be sitting on her soon to be husbands face like it was my own pony. She needed to tighten up. I would never go around befriending bitches that were my husband's friends.

"No, I believe there's more to it, a lot more to it. You're the girl in the tattoo." She smirked.

I smirked back, I was pleasantly surprised with her observation and the mural on his body that would never be removed.

"Good observation, but what does that had to do with me and you being friends?" I asked.

I don't have any friends Rose. It would be nice to have a girl's night or something. Don't you think?"

"It's Tru." She was getting a little too comfortable.

"I'm sorry, I thought Damien called you Rose."

"That's an old nickname that doesn't get used often, just call me Tru."

"Ok, so what do you say to being friends?" she asked excited and I hated to be the one to shoot her down but that's exactly what was about to happen. I didn't need any news friends, especially any as shallow as her.

"You mean to tell me that a rich, established socialite such as yourself doesn't have any friends?" this bitch was getting on my nerves already. If she wanted to keep an eye on me she didn't have to.

"Not any real ones, they all hang out because they want spotlight. You don't seem to care about that. I mean you get to wear the Boho chic look and not have to worry about being in the next article."

"I'll think about it," I had no desire to politic or hang out with Erica. But I did have something up my sleeve. "Erica, you know Ryan, don't you?"

Her eyes went up, you know playing as if she was thinking of what Ryan I was speaking of. *Nice try*, I thought to myself. I wanted to say, you know the Ryan you've been paying and probably secretly sleeping around with. But I didn't, I allowed her a moment to play with me and my time.

"The scientist?" she asked.

"Yeah, Ryan, I thought you guys were friends or at least associates." I sat directly across from her on the edge of my desk. I was able to see the slight perspiration and the twitch of her eye. Poor thing was losing it.

"Well yeah, but that's family stuff. I mean real friends that like to shop, grab lunch and have girl talk." She smiled.

"Erica, I don't think you want to be friends. You want to keep an eye on me and Thorn. I can assure you that you've wasted all that precious time coming to the slums to visit." Times up. I tried really hard to take her seriously. Me and Erica would never be friends. We would never enjoy the same things. And we would never have anything real to share.

"You think this is about Damien?" she asked looking at her perfect manicure.

"I know this is about Thorn," I reiterated calling him by something she would never call him by. "I knew this at the party. Secure women don't have to push up or make secret visits. Tell me does Damien know you are here?"

"No, he doesn't, but since you brought it up," she said now standing to her feet directly in front of me. It looked like we were about to duel. "Stand down Tru or Rose whatever your name is. Damien and I are set to be married and I won't let some college fling tear that apart or stop that. Do you understand?"

"Erica, let me tell you something." See, now she had me fucked up completely. I understand exactly what she was saying, but I also didn't care. "I understand the dynamic of your relationship with my friend, Thorn, but I can assure that I would never want to see anything happen to him. So, let's just clear this up. Stop whatever games you are playing, and I go away. If not, 'Hey, best friend' is what you will hear and see every time you turn around. I will hunt anyone down and do damage if they bring harm to him. Now do I make myself clear?"

"Crystal," she replied.

"Great, this was such a positive and productive visit. See your way out." I said going to sit back at my desk. I had work to do. The nerve of her to come down was commendable but I was unbothered. Her threats were dead and held no value with me. I was a real bully. I was really about that life of ruining and ending people. Light treading is the only advice I had for her. This wasn't a game she wanted to play with me. She would be the next and only target. I would eat, sleep, breath her demise.

137

More Secrets

"We need to meet ASAP," I said into the phone speaking with Ryan. Tru wasn't going to play fair and I could sense that the moment I stepped foot in her office. Her tone, her demeanor all of it was off. It was like she knew something I didn't. That didn't sit well with me. Ryan assured me that she was the one for the job and now it seemed that I was the one on the chopping block. My only intention was to make sure we were on the same page.

I knew all about her relationship with Damien and I tried hard to play it off, but it was clear my poker face wasn't strong enough to throw her off. The minute I seen her at the dinner, I recognized her. After Damien scolded me at his family's party I knew there was more to them that anyone had ever let on. I didn't care that Damien had feelings for someone else. I didn't want to marry Damien any more than he wanted to marry me. I just couldn't mess this up for my family. I had already had enough scandals that no one could speak about. I had to redeem myself.

"Come to the pub," he said disconnecting.

The pub wasn't far from Tru's office, so it took me no time to get there. I walked in and searched for Ryan. I didn't see him, so I quietly sat at the bar and waited. Checking my emails and our ranking. We were so close to winning the race. We just had to hang on for a few more weeks.

"Hey Emilio, let me get my usual." I heard come from beside me. Her voice was velvety and smooth. I tried my hardest not to look her way but her soft hand grazed my hand and I couldn't fight the feeling it gave me. Looking to my left, I came face to face with a set of blue eyes. It looked like she had the ocean trapped in her eyes. Flowing and crashing. She looked dangerous and yet so beautiful.

"Indigo, long time no see." Emilio said excitedly. Even her name was beautiful. It fit her. Her long legs seem to go on for days and her hair that long blonde ponytail went on for hours.

"Who's your friend?" she asked.

"I'm Erica," I said extending my hand with a smile. Her hand touched mine and I felt it again. It was so powerful that I felt like I touched a light socket. I pulled back quickly. This was bad for me and I couldn't possibly stay here with this type of temptation.

"Nice to meet you. New to the area?"

"Uh no, I'm supposed to be meeting a friend here, but he hasn't arrived yet." I said nervously.

"Let me play you in a game of pool, you know to buy the time." She offered.

"I don't know how to play." I admitted. She was so strong, I could tell she grew up differently than I had. She had a biker feel to her. Tattoos littered her body, piecing's in her face and ears. Her combat boots, and tight skinny jeans were a contrast to her soft features.

"Too easy, ill teach you. Come on."

Sliding off the stool and grabbing my spritzer, I followed her to the pool table. The nerves were setting in and I caught myself constantly surveying the area. A lot of people didn't know the side of me that got me in trouble and in the position I was in now. You see, Damien didn't have to marry me, I had another sister that was perfect for this type of shit. I was the black sheep, much like Ryan. This marriage was an opportunity to save face.

But smelling her sweet perfume and feel her warm skin touch my skin was a sweet escape. I felt myself not caring anymore about saving face. I wanted my old life back. The life that allowed me to be who I was. The lesbian life. I loved women. I loved women to much that it got in some compromising positions. My family hadn't the secret life and that's why they were marrying me off to the most eligible bachelor.

"You've got good posture," she whispered in my ear. I felt a chill run down my spine as I sat bent over the pool table. Her hand was guiding my back to keep me in place and it felt like heaven. My thighs began to quake as she kicked my legs open wider. I inhaled sharply, because I was playing with fire. I just knew I was.

Searching for Something

Erica had to be a fool to think she would be able to walk out of my office and not have me follow her. I was a private investigator what did she think her visit would do. It didn't scare me it made my suspicions peak.

The pub wasn't far from my office which was good. It was a small walk especially since I knew where she was going. While she made her grand speech, I slipped a listening device into her purse. She was so careless. Whoever sent her was just as much of an amateur.

I watched from the window and was surprised to see Indigo back in town. She was what my mother would call a "bulldiker" I personally hated that term, but it fit. She was such a beautiful soul but rigid at the same time. She made it known that she liked women and that's why she hadn't been around in some time. In true Raven's Pointe fashion, they ran her off with their anti-gay propaganda, brandishing stakes and torches because she was a lesbian. But it was clear she was back and preying on her next target. But as I watched and snapped photos it didn't look like this one would be a victim of being turned out. It looked like Erica was already there. I laughed because I missed that sign. She was smiling and inhaling roughly. It looked like she was in true bliss with a woman behind her and touching her a little intimately.

This trip to the pub was getting even better as I watched Ryan come from the back. He looked disgusted with the sight before him. His face was tight, and his eyebrow raised. Yeah he was upset or confused.

"Erica, seriously" he said in a hushed tone. I was thankful for my ability to hear, well when I wanted to. It wasn't my strongest power, but it came in handy.

"Oh, Ryan, lighten up she was just teaching me to play pool." She replied.

"Yeah, Ryan, lighten up." Indigo poked.

"Erica, follow me." He snapped.

Watching them disappear I made my way into the pub to speak with Indigo. She had this gift. The gift of knowing more about your sexuality than you did. There was a reason she went for Erica and I needed to know why that was. I wasn't concerned about hearing the conversation between her and Ryan. It was being recorded as they hashed it out.

"Welcome back to town stranger," I said sitting on the pool table. She was a beautiful woman, but I just wasn't into women. She tried her hand and failed miserably but that didn't keep us from being friends.

"Well, well look who we have here. The baddest bitch in the land." She joked coming in for a hug.

"Indigo, what the hell are you doing here?" I asked. She was back in the flesh as if she didn't have a care in the world. I wondered why? Most that left didn't come back, finding solace in another place with less judgement and rules.

"My mother, she's sick. I had to come back whether they want me here or not."

"I'm so sorry to hear that. How long you been back?"

"About a month, I've been keeping a low profile." She shrugged.

"The pub isn't a low profile, Indi."

"I know but I'm lonely, so I had to make an exception." She winked.

"Who is she?" I asked as if I hadn't just watched her grope and struggle snuggle with Erica.

"I don't kiss and tell, you know that."

That was a subliminal hit at me, but I dodged that shit instantly. I liked men and it wouldn't change because she had asked for the millionth time.

"I saw you all cozy with one and only Erica Wainwright, is that the next victim?"

"No victim, I'm looking for love, Tru. I'm getting older and it's time for us to get the life we want to. You know your boy, is fighting for us to get some rights."

That was a shock to me, I hadn't seen that as a part of his campaign. But more power to him if he could for once change the mind of Avia.

"I wish you and him luck. How do you know when to approach, you know another woman?"

"They don't make eye contact, they treat me the same way they'd treat a man. Coy! But her, she's already been there. I could tell."

That's all I wanted to hear, I just needed Indi to confirm my suspicions. Now I had more work to dig up. If Erica was a lesbian it meant her family was probably making her marry Thorn. But what I couldn't figure out is why she would want him to lose the race or not be senator if he was fighting for her to be her true self.

"Welcome back and I'll be praying for your mom, good seeing you," I said making my exit from the pub. Work for the day was over. I was going home pleased with the work from today.

Nothing but Love

Making it home, I kicked off my shoes and laid down on the couch. My mind was racing trying to make sense of it all. Erica's part of this shit show didn't make sense. And then on top of trying to solve this mystery, my thoughts were on the greatest love story of all time, me and Thorn. After being in his realm, I had the strongest urge to see him, touch him and hear his voice. I planned to take a nap in hopes that the residue would be removed once I woke up.

Slowly falling in to a deep slumber, vivid images of our wedding played in my head. *I was in a white off shoulder flowy gown. It was just my style. The white and red roses covered the venue. We were in his mother's backyard, the white carpet seemed to go on for ages. The guest were all in awe as the stared at me standing with my father on my arm. The rose decorated ballet length veil covered my face, it felt beat to the gawds but light. On my feet were the rose gold Valentino bow lace shoe. That confused me, I wasn't a label whore. Maybe Damien turned me into one.*

"You look beautiful princess," my dad whispered patting my hand. I felt us floating towards the front.

We were so close to the alter. My heart rate sped up at the realization that my happy ending would soon be coming. I would finally be able to be Mrs. Damien Thorn. This was all I had ever hoped for.

I could see Damien's face, but it was distorted. He looked like a robot. He wasn't happy, he wasn't himself, but as I got closer his face started to look like the real him, it got clearer and back into focus.

"Hear ye, hear ye," the officiator said as I approached. "Who gives this bride away?"

"I do," my dad said. As he ushered me to Damien, a force held me back. I couldn't move my feet. I was planted in place.

"Thorn grab me," it didn't matter how hard he pulled I wouldn't move. I started to panic. "Help!" I screamed for someone to help me get to my final destination.

"Please!" I begged. I was begging for someone to help me get back to Thorn. The more I begged the further away I got. "No please don't do this, we were so close." I screamed.

"Rose, wake up. You're dreaming." I heard from above me. Slowly opening my eyes, the tears flowed. It felt real and it scared me. It scared me to think that once again he would be ripped away from me.

"Thorn what are you doing here?" I asked attempting to still my busy spirit.

"I needed to see you," he said sitting at my feet. I looked up to read his face. I felt like we were opening a box we wouldn't be able to close. Maybe the dream made me feel that way. The idea of being so close to being together, and then it saddened and angered me. Maybe we weren't meant to be.

"That dream was crazy. Something bad is going to happen and I don't know if we can save one another." I said sitting up and facing him. I wanted to see his face when I told him that maybe we needed to not see each other. The plan would have to be a separate attack. "I think we are being watched."

My dreams had never been as vivid as this one. I had a hunch and I was rarely wrong. Whoever was watching us was careful not to get close knowing I would sense it.

"What if I said I really didn't care?" he asked.

"I'd say you were crazy. You have to care Damien. This is all you've ever wanted, don't be foolish." I fussed.

"Don't you be foolish. We made a mistake back then, I should have fought more for you, but I didn't. I want to now."

"I can't let you do that, you need to leave and never come back. Let me do this alone. When it's time, you will know."

"No, you found something didn't you?" he asked with a hopeful look. I didn't want him involved anymore. I couldn't risk something happening to him or his chances. I believed that there was a way to still get him in office in tact without the old ball and chain. I needed him to trust me and let me do what I did best.

"I don't want you involved. It's simple. Do you understand that this is bigger than you taking office?" I was sure he wasn't thinking of all the things they would do to him. They would blackball him, ruining his image, tarnish his name, and possibly have him killed.

"I don't give a fuck about that shit anymore. I can't stop thinking about you and what we had. What I want." He said standing to his feet. "You've made me better with one night, I can't lose that again."

"Dame, you need to speak with your mother."

"For what? She doesn't care what I really want. She's never going to accept us."

"This isn't about me and you. When it's our time, it will be our time."

"Rose for real stop playing with me. Ain't nobody better for you than me. I still think I know what's best for you." He laughed.

"Listen, I'll come with you. She needs to know what's going on. This affects them also." I hated to be the one to burst bubbles when it came to people I actually cared about, but I had to do it. Darlene needed to know that she was and had been being played like a flute. They didn't see her family as equal, they were pawns like the rest of us.

"Fine," he agreed. "If this doesn't work we do it my way." I looked at him with so much love, nothing but love. Just a few days ago, I hated the thought of him. But now I was just pleased that I finally had my friend back. I prayed this visit with his mother went well or shit was going to hit the fan and soon.

Wicked Witch

Pulling up to my mother's house something felt off. Or maybe I was just worried that she would make up some excuse to protect those she thought where her friends. Either way, I was leery of involving my mom, but at the end of the day, she needed to know that my run for senator would be over soon. They wouldn't allow me to win and they damn sure wouldn't let me stay in office long. I didn't know what Rose uncovered but I knew it had to be big if she wanted me to involve my mother.

"Ma," I yelled letting myself in.

"Back here, love." Walking into my mom's study, I looked around and she looked terrible. Her face held pain and sadness. Rose was close on my heels. "What is she doing here? With you?" she asked with her nose turned up.

"Ma, you need to chill and accept the fact that Rose will always have a place in my heart. You've been played ma," I spoke sitting down on the golden antique chair.

"What do you mean?" she asked turning to face us. "Don't tell me you've allowed her to weasel her way back into your life. Damien you just refuse to listen."

"Darlene, you need to shut up the hell up and listen for one damn minute. Damien is being watched. In fact, I've been asked to bring Damien down. Ravens Pointe does not want him to win the senate. His fiancé's family is paying the secret society to keep him from winning."

Rose then slammed down a tape recorder on the table and pressed play. Maybe it was a good idea to bring her. She wasn't about to take my mommas shit and that made me want to bend her over the desk like I should've done years ago. Listening to the recording, cancelled

149

that thought. I was furious and disappointed with the lengths people would go to to see me fail.

"Ryan, she's not going to do what we asked." I heard Erica mention. "I went to visit her, and she is prepared to protect Damien."

Why didn't she tell me about this visit? I knew there was a reason she was acting strange when she came home today. I paid it no mind, because women were hot and cold a lot, especially Erica. I could barely read her moods and most of the time I didn't try because I wasn't invested.

"She can't do that, she is a member and risking her own life not following through. Maybe you misunderstood. No one told you to go there anyway starting shit. Listen, play your part until I tell you something different." Ryan whispered.

"Yeah, well I'm paying you to keep him out of Senate. Figure out something else because this doesn't seem to be working right now. You should have seen the way she looked at me when she warned me to cut out whatever I had planned." She scolded. I was shocked to learn that it was Erica behind all of this. She was a damn good actor.

"Erica, it's a shame that you don't understand how this works. Even if you don't become the senator's wife you still won't be accepted as a lesbian. That little shit you pulled out there was unacceptable."

"A lesbian?" I asked looking at Rose. I was floored at the revelation of Erica being a lesbian. She nodded her head, just as shocked as me.

"Ryan, let me tell you something. I am sick of living a lie and this is my way to not have to worry about this shit anymore I can live my own damn life. Do what I pay you for."

"I slipped a recorder on her when she came to "warn me" about you. Damien you need to be careful," She begged. "They aren't playing fair."

150

"Ma, this is what you want, not me." I was irritated that anyone would go to such lengths to ruin something positive. I had big plans for RP and now I had to watch my back. Me and Erica weren't in love, but I felt we had a mutual love for each other. But now I see that I had to watch my back. All she had to do was be honest about what she wanted, and we could have figured something out.

"We've all been pawns in the game before Damien. You will be senator, and you will marry Erica. This doesn't prove anything." I heard my mother say.

"Excuse me?" I asked. I was hoping I was hearing her incorrectly. She couldn't possibly want me to continue with this run for senate after what we all just heard. I knew politics held some level of getting your hands dirty, but my life wasn't something to play with.

"Power is the only thing that matters. You will be senator, and I will see to it. Rose stop the investigation and let me handle the rest."

"I'm not marrying Erica, I never wanted to, and that sentiment is still the same. Handle what you can." I advised.

"Damien, you will marry Erica, we have to get the power balanced. It's always been the law of the land. I understand that you love her, but she has no power and no way to make a change."

"Her name is Rose, and I allowed you to tear us apart before, but I won't do it now. Its ultimately my choice to run for senator, so make it happen but cancel the wedding." I demanded that the wedding be canceled and quickly. There was no way I was marrying Erica. Both of our hands were being forced and it was best that someone had the balls to end the bullshit. I wouldn't take part in the charade anymore. If winning the senate came with lies, it wasn't for me.

"Fine, I'll call you soon," she agreed. I didn't stand a chance surviving with all the big players involved. Erica and her father weren't on the same page. This was ridiculous, and this was the part of politics I refused to take a part in. If I married Erica, a scandal would come soon after and that would carry the same weight if it was my own damn scandal. This shit was dead and over with. I couldn't wait for it to be over, so I could once and for all go back to being Thorn.

A week later......

Standing in the park, I let the breeze toss my hair all around. It was a nice day; the coffee was bringing me to life. I needed it. Sleep hadn't found me since the night with Damien. It's taken me so long to grasp what happened that night and everything that had transpired over the last week. I couldn't figure out if Ryan set me up or if Ryan knew how strong our love was. I hated him more than I've ever hated him.

I was furious with Damien for signing up to be one of Ryan's lab rats. That was stupid. The one person that held your future in his hands had dirt that wouldn't blow over so well with the community. Ryan's research was supposed to be monumental, but now I see it just another way to oppress us. Vivid images came back from the day he asked for my help. I said yes without second thought. I desired to be different. I was still mourning and grieving the loss of Damien. I was so weak....

"Rose, wait up" I heard Ryan running to catch up to me before I went into the mess hall.

"I don't know where Colleen is," I replied. He always thought we had to know each other's location and that wasn't true. Colleen was her own woman and it wasn't my job to keep up with her.

"No that's not it. I need a big favor from you. Can we talk in private?"

Staring at him suspiciously, I couldn't imagine what I, the black girl who got lucky, could do for Ryan, the rich and powerful, "I don't scrub toilets." It was somewhat of a joke; we were beneath Ryan and he pretended so well that he cared for us equally. He failed miserably. He thought because he had one black friend it meant he fucked with us all. Big lie and no facts.

"Don't do that, you know I'm not like that," he said, trying to convince himself.

"What is it?"

"Follow me, I've been working on something and I can't tell you here," Again, I looked at him suspiciously. Ryan was a handsome guy, but he was so damn strange.

"You're socially awkward ass bet not be on some other shit. I'm smart but I will kick your ass," I warned.

"Oh, come on,"

I stupidly followed him into his lab, and the smell that hit my nostrils almost made me turn around. But as he started talking about the shit he was into, I was intrigued. Ryan had rats, chickens and some had been genetically modified. Scary shit but I was interested.

"You see, Tru; this is the next big thing. I need to test my shit on you."

"What's in it for me?" I asked. I had nothing to lose, but I also wasn't about to become a science project without nothing in return.

"Five thousand dollars, and hopefully super powers," he shrugged.

I could use that type of money, and I would also love to have super powers, who wouldn't. The ability to fly, jump, save was enticing, "What are the risk?"

"No different from anything else. What do you say?"

I sat and weighed my options. How could it be? I had so much to gain, it could take the things I wanted to do so far. I could open my PI firm and be ahead of the game.

"I'll do it," I foolishly agreed. "When do we start?"

"We can start today, its Friday night. I only need a few days to get you started and watch over you."

"Ok, do I need to do anything?" I asked.

"No, just take this gown and change."

Doing as I was told I went into the bathroom slipped the hospital gown on and said a minor prayer before I allowed this fool to inject me with all kinds of shit. I knew I was probably doing this for all the wrong reasons. But hell, I had nothing to lose.

"I'm ready," I said emerging from the bathroom. I was led into a small operating room. I started to freak out with all the lights and needles around. It was too late to turn back now and plus I could really use 5,000 dollars. This was my senior year and soon I would have to navigate life on my own with no financial aid making life easier.

"Rose, listen this is confidential, I request that you sign a NDA, this can't be talked about."

I signed the paper not reading a damn word on it. It was college, hell I was tired of reading shit. That was the damn I was sworn into secrecy. I laid on my stomach as Ryan got started. He hooked the IV up, connected a heart monitor and applied cold betadine to my back I flinched from the cool feeling. My mind was racing not sure what the hell would take place after this was done and what the procedure would even be like. I had never had surgery before and I was scared shitless.

"This isn't going to feel good, but I will put you under for most of it, count back from ten." He instructed.

"Ten, nine, eigh"

I should have done my research. I should have used my damn brain before I made a decision that couldn't be reversed. I allowed Ryan to play God and alter my body. I was sick as a damn dog and scarred up completely after the testing. I almost flunked out of school due to being sick and being weird. It worked but I didn't receive a pamphlet of things to do and not to do.

"Any news?"

"None other than, I think the hole is his bride to be," I only mentioned that to see Ryan's reaction. "something's suspect about Erica," his face contorted, and jaw flinched. His poker face was trash as well.

"How do you know about Erica?"

"It's my damn job, please explain?" I said facing him. His line of questioning made no sense. It was my damn duty to know any and everything about Thorn even who he was fucking.

"It wasn't in the file," he stated like that mattered. It was the beauty of my job. I found out what was left out of the file. How stupid could he be to think I wouldn't find out. Not to mention if the file had all the things they needed to bring him down there was no need for my line of work.

"Ryan, my job as a PI is to find the hidden shit, what's this really about?" I asked needing to know now more than ever what I signed up for. Something was being hidden from me, and normally that was when I declined the job. No skeletons of your own or it would completely disintegrate the nature of my work. If I exposed your mate, or employee and you had shit with you, I wouldn't work with you. I needed to know everything about you and the subject. It was just how I worked.

"We've had this conversation Tru," he was fidgeting and wiping imaginary lint from his jacket. I wanted to kick him in the balls, for bringing me in this shit.

"Well let me do my damn job," I walked off I had a busy day today. I had real fucking work to do. Ryan had agitated me and had no idea. He had better be thankful, I somewhat had control over myself. Walking back to my car, I could feel the anger rising. I didn't like being played or being a tangled in a web of bullshit.

Luckily my office wasn't too far away, I was running late. Traffic was crazy and then I had the worse attitude. The coffee I had earlier wasn't doing the trick anymore. Walking in, I could see Colleen and my nine o'clock appointment. It was Khalil. Today must have been piss Tru off day, because everyone was irritating and frustrating me. The games had to end and soon.

"Khalil," I offered, leading to my office. My office was spacious, and it overlooked the city. It was the high rise that made me fall in love with it. It was lovely, and it fit me. Authentic brick covered the walls, with hints of girly touches. My desk was large and made of glass. It was very modern. However, the eye sore before me cancelled all that joy out.

"Tru, how are you? You look splendid," he said.

This was why me and Khalil would never be. He was full of shit. I looked like last week. I wore the same shit all the time and the same colors. Khalil was a fine-looking man, but he had yet to pick a damn side. His broad shoulders, bald head, and perfect goatee were some of the features that had me open at one point but it was his mouth that turned me off.

"What do you want?" I asked getting to the point. I could've slept in had I known he was my nine o'clock appointment. Matter of fact, I'd be getting into Colleen's ass for this.

"Straight to the point, huh?"

"Yeah, so get to it," Khalil and I had something at one point. I can't recall what that something was, but it was something. It was weak moment for me that ended abruptly. But the smirk that graced his smooth caramel skin was letting me know that it wasn't over for him. In that moment that something hit me, it was sex and vulnerability. I was attempting to move on from the disaster Damien caused and he was there waiting with that same smile and good dick. The irony, but I wouldn't be easily persuaded this time. It was perfect timing, as I was still struggling with the revived flame of me and Thorn. But this time, I wouldn't run from the feeling or try and mask it with someone else.

"I miss you, that's why I'm here," he adjusted his stance and his intense glare did nothing for me. I scooted closer, unfazed.

"Come again?" I heard him perfectly fine, but I needed to hear it again. I needed to hear the lies again. I loved when people felt the need to lie to me, right in my face.

"I miss us, we had good times, right?"

"We had good sex, that's about it. You talk but no action follows." Khalil was a lawyer; it was his job to talk and feed lies. He was exceptional at it, but it was my job to sift through the lies. His lies eventually caught up with him. The promises of being something more, the promises of making me his wife, the promises of being there for me quickly faded once he realized I wasn't one to conform.

"Not true, and you know it," he said playing confused. It was so true and that I did know. What we had ended years ago, and I hadn't looked back and neither had he until now. We saw each other often and the most I got from him was a head nod.

"Why now?" I asked although it wouldn't persuade me one way or the other. We weren't compatible, we didn't believe in the same things, and he wasn't authentic. I hadn't dated much but I knew what I wanted in my potential mate. It wasn't Khalil. My future mate needed to have a backbone, be authentic, and true to themselves. I required truth, because that's what I brought to the table. I had my own funds, my own life and my standards. I didn't need anyone that wanted to impose theirs upon me. In a nutshell, I wanted Thorn, the old Thorn. If I got that back, it would be game over for any other man that came.

"We aren't getting any younger, Tru," he explained.

"So, your biological clock is ticking, and you want me of all people to make it stop?" I wanted to laugh in his smug face. It was no coincidence he was here. I knew what he was trying to do. "I see it now, pop out six kids, be a doting wife, host dinner parties, and fuck you senseless and then you love me for life. Sounds terrible." Instead of laughing in his face, I would just mock him and make him feel small like he did everyone else.

"Tru, who else is out there for you?"

"Oh, so you think I'm desperate?" There was the Khalil I knew. The one that couldn't help but put himself on a pedestal. He never allowed anyone else to do. This is why he would always be single; he didn't know when to shut up and stop thinking so much of himself. I was all for self-love and all that good shit, but I couldn't deal with him convincing himself he was more than what he was.

"No, but I am. I'm desperately wanting to make this work." He was such a fool. Why would anyone want to deal with someone that didn't want to deal with them? "Let's try again."

"I think it's really sweet of you, but you know we would only be fooling ourselves. Khalil what we had wasn't love it was convenience." I hated to be the one that broke his heart and dropped him down a few notches, but someone had to do it. His tight ass wasn't the most eligible bachelor; he was damn near psychotic and he was a chauvinistic bitch. No one and I do mean no one wanted to deal with that. And to add to the bullshit, he was one of Ryan's closest do-boys, passing up on this clown was a no brainer for me.

"Tru, no one is checking for you so why not make it easy on me." He chuckled.

Now that was the green light to laugh in his face and say fuck his little feelings. This was the Khalil that turned me off. A fucking man child at its finest. Couldn't get what he wanted or the answer he was searching for and now it was time for him to dim my light. Try again bitch.

"That's so funny, and you are probably correct, so again why are you in my office, smelling good, freshly shaved, and in that suit you know I love?" I asked leaning back attempting to break the tension. If he kept up the games, this would only be the pregame show. I hated to get disrespectful, but I would if he attempted to waste any more of my time.

"I'll be back at six to pick you up for dinner."

Standing to my feet, I stared at him like he was some maniac. "No, I don't want to go to dinner with you. Who's checking for me remember?"

"I am," he stated standing himself. I wanted to bum rush him, but instead I just stared at him "now be ready to go when I arrive." He left. He just dropped that demand and left like it was nothing. Like I didn't have a right to an opinion.

Rushing to the elevator, he was already gone. "Colleen, what the hell, why didn't you warn me that Khalil was coming?"

"He said it was urgent, and plus I like Khalil for you." She shrugged. A fucking shrug was all she gave me like that was enough to excuse her lapse of judgement.

"It wasn't urgent and now he expects me to go to dinner with him. This is bullshit," I was so mad and angry that I managed to kick my door off the hinges. Pacing the floor, Colleen came in with that look on her face. The look of 'I know somethings up'. Not making eye contact with her, I couldn't tell her what was going on because I honestly had no clue how to feel or how to process what was brewing in my life.

The way Thorn looked at me the other night. The way we laughed like old times; it was magical and downright foolish of me. I woke up that next morning with a smile on my face. I jumped out of bed ready to get shit started and get the ball rolling. It was like I was floating on clouds. It was the way it always was with him. I was beaming to my office and I know it was nothing but the love we shared resurfacing.

"You slept with him?" She guessed.

"Hell no, but shit's different." It really wasn't. He was still running for Senate, and he was still expected to be with someone other than me. I had to save him from the biggest mistake he would ever make in his life. If I didn't, he would live a life of sadness and despair. I couldn't let my friend go through that, for a title that wouldn't last long. If he won, he would be assassinated. They would never let him live in peace. It didn't matter that he was deserving or that he was the perfect man for the job. His skin tone and the nature of his campaign wouldn't allow them to give him or black people a fucking break. We deserved him and the break he so badly wanted for us.

"How is it different? He is still picking everyone and everything over you."

I was standing still, but my heart was still moving with the will to save him. Save him for me. It was me he was supposed to love. I forgave him, because he did what he thought was best. I felt his presence even when he wasn't around now. Touching him that night was like adding fuel to a fire. He was everywhere now, in my mind, in my thoughts and back in my bones.

"You wouldn't understand, and I'm not about to make you understand. Leave it alone," she had to leave it alone. I didn't want to run down the past week to her or the shit that I found out. Ryan was still her brother and she still owed him some level of allegiance. I blamed him for putting me in this situation, but right now I didn't know who I could trust. Ryan wasn't playing fair, and I knew that was

161

why Khalil was here and why he was attempting to glide back into a place that wasn't vacant.

"Just don't get hurt, Damien is and will always be about his own personal gain. Don't become another casualty," she muttered, leaving me to my own thoughts.

Swiveling in my chair, I stared out at the city. The hustle and bustle never stopped. My minded drifted. I didn't want to pass the torch to someone else. I wanted to fall in love with him over and over again. People made mistakes, and if he realized that, maybe there was hope for us. We could finally make it right. I needed to come up with a clever plan to allow Damien to get what he wanted and deserved, but also have me. The trick was I didn't even know if he wanted that. Was I really willing to go that length to see him happy again and be possibly left out in the cold by myself? Could I afford to become another casualty of the Damien Thorn legacy? The questions I had could only be cleared up by one person and that was Damien. I needed to see him and right away.

"Hold my calls. I'm gone for the day,"

Leaving my office, something felt off. It scared me, because I felt the change come about. It was broad daylight and I had nothing to conceal me. Nothing to shield me. Walking down the street, was uncomfortable. Picking up my pace, I had to get to my car. But as I headed in the direction of the parking garage, I could hear screams and pleas. Now the forces within me were leading me past the garage and down the alley.

"Give me my baby back," a lady screamed. Shaking my head, I attempted to rid myself of the voices. I could feel my ears tingling and my pupils dilating. I couldn't turn around even if I wanted to. This wasn't me this was someone else controlling my emotions and my movements. Jumping from trash can to trash can, I landed right in front of the captor. In his arms was a small child, wrapped in a blanket, crying.

"Help please, call the police!" she yelled.

"Mind your business, freak." He screamed at me. I was so sick of being called a freak, but what other word was it for someone that could do all that I could do. I was a freak of nature and needed to accept it.

"No need for name calling. Give her the baby back and I can do just that." There was always a chance to do the right thing, I just hoped he took it. Because if not today would be a bad day because I wasn't in the mood and Khalil had me riled up.

"No way, lady. This baby has been paid for get your own."

"I gave you the money back, please" the mother was still begging, and I was disappointed in her for attempting to sell an innocent baby to this low life. Why make a baby that you couldn't afford? It was absurd the shit people did for money.

"I told you double for the deal to be scrapped."

"I don't have double. I made a mistake. Just give me my baby back," she cried harder. Her hair was matted to her head, her nails were dirty, and her clothes reeked of trash and mildew. The baby may have been better off with someone but I wasn't the one to judge. With all that I had going on there was no way I could critic someone else and the shit they had going on.

"Please, Julian please," she begged more. His mind wasn't changing and enough was enough. It was clear that I would have to expose myself to get this mother her baby back. I had to act quickly. He was backing up to the van.

"I'll give you five seconds to return the baby. If not, me and you will have to discuss other arrangements," I said moving closer to the van, I ripped the door from its hinges. Holding it in my hand, "you see, I am a freak, and I can't let you leave with this baby." There was no telling what life this baby would live, if I let him take her. The mother would never see her again.

"What are you?" he asked.

"Your worst nightmare. Five seconds are up," I responded, kicking him in the knees and punching him in the face. He was strong but not stronger than me. As he dropped to the ground like a sack of potatoes, he dropped the baby on the ground, the mother was able to grab the baby and flee. Now it was just me and him.

Grunting as he stood to his feet, I kicked him in the ribs. He still wouldn't drop. Charging at me, he threw my body up against a trash can. Headbutting him, he staggered back, but came charging at me again. I blocked his punch but couldn't miss the punch to the gut.

"You hit like a bitch," I confessed wiping my mouth. Understanding that he wanted a fight I removed my jacket. Tossing it to the floor, I stood my stance and prepared for a battle. This guy wasn't going easily, and now I knew it was about his ego. The baby was gone.

"I'm going to kill you, and then I'm going to kill her. You just cost me ten-grand."

Running up the wall and landing behind him, I grabbed him by the neck, "Good luck with that," choking him until he became heavy and his breathing slowed. I dropped him and that's when I realized that cameras were out, and people were staring at me. I was surrounded by onlookers, some cheering, some whispering and some on the phone. Attempting to get away, I climbed the fire escaped and jumped building to building. I needed to get far away for a minute. Soon it would be all on the news and I'd be exposed and hunted.

The Interrogation

I could hear the sirens closing in and I wasn't even sure what I was running from. I hadn't done anything wrong. I saved a baby from being kidnapped. That was something to be celebrated. I knew they wouldn't see it that way so attempting to get ahead of the bullshit I walked into the Police Station.

"Freeze, put your hands on your head," I heard them yell. My face was all over the news and I knew they had come up with some story of me being a danger to society. Hell, maybe I was.

Hands above my head, I allowed porky the pig to place the cuffs on me and read me my rights. I hated this shit hole, but it was the only way I could see what they had on me and what they wanted. I wouldn't stay long, I could break out but first I needed to know what I was up against.

"Don't be so rough asshole," I said as they led me to an interrogation room. It was freezing in here and I'm sure this was their tactic. It wouldn't work. I was the one in here on my own accord. We would play by my rules.

"Wait here, while we get the detective." Porky said securing me to the rail on the table. I thought long and hard about what I would say and what my tactic would be to get out of here safely and cleared. I'm sure it wouldn't happen how I planned but I was prepared for whatever they came in here with. If I didn't like what was being said I would lawyer up and call the one person I didn't want to call, Khalil.

The door opened and in walked Detective DeVito and Detective Jones, both equal part idiot and asshole. I knew they would be on the case and I knew Detective Jones would be thrilled to see my face considering I almost cost her her job for stealing from the people she arrested.

"Look who we have here, Trulicity, the baddest PI known to Raven's Pointe." She joked. I smirked ready to go back and forth with a thief that refused to be held accountable.

"Hey, still stealing from the innocent until proven guilty?" I asked. That shut her up quickly. I'm sure all of her colleagues didn't know about her indiscretions. She had better played nice or we would have a day of airing out dirty laundry.

"Mind telling us what happened out there?" DeVito asked.

"Just being a good citizen, I don't understand the problem."

"Well there some videos going on out there about you assaulting an innocent man attempting to pick his kid up for visitation." He responded.

"Is that what they are saying?" I laughed.

"Yeah, you broke that man's nose."

"Well that was the plan, am I being charged?"

"Depends on what you tell us, Tru. That was a pretty impressive jump you did out there." He smirked.

"Yeah, I've been eating my Wheaties. Now let's talk seriously, am I being charged?" I wasn't going to continue to go back and forth. If they wanted to know something that had better started asking before I took my chances and escaped this wretched place. It was clear I wasn't going to get any information out of them.

"Actually, it's your lucky day, the ABI is picking up the case. Something about you being a mutant. Enjoy your day, Tru." They both laughed as the left the room. Sweat started to form. This was what I didn't want to happen. But now that I knew I had to get out of her and quickly.

Calm my nerves, I focused on getting my arm released. Fist clenched I pulled and freed myself. The rail was still dangling from my arm as I jumped from my seat. Looking back, I had to make sure no one was coming or privy to what I was doing. Rushing to the door, I listened to see if anyone was coming or if I could hear the ABI coming. I didn't hear anything and that was my que to get the fuck out of dodge before I was moved to a facility I would never get out of.

The window was covered with steel rods, but it would be nothing to bend them and break the window. I had to move quickly because there was no quiet way to make this happen. Scooting the chair over the window, I stood on top and pulled at the bars until they began to pop out of the window. Taking the pole attached to my arm I busted the window as the door flew open. The ABI wasted no time getting here, it was as if they knew I would be captured. Without wasting time I slipped through the window.

"Stop," I heard one yell. I wasn't stopping until I got out of town.

"Sir, she escaped," I heard as I stayed crouched down out of the window. I had a small window of time to make it off of the precinct grounds. It wouldn't be long before they sent the troops looking for me. Lacing up my boots, tossing my hood over my head and zipping my jacket up I took off running in the opposite direction of the footsteps.

Finally Home......

Sneaking in to my apartment, I started packing. I need to get out of town for a little while. I had no idea where I would go, but I had to go somewhere and fast. My worst fear had come true. I was attempting to not freak out, but it wasn't working. The idea of being labelled and confined scared me. Then thoughts of my parents and the things they would go through had me on edge. I wanted to kick, cry and scream because this was not how imagined my day going. I was going to get with Thorn and make sure this was what he wanted. I knew emotions made people move hastily and I didn't want that for him or me again. Grabbing what I could the news started to play.

Breaking News,

"This video of a supernatural woman has surfaced. In the video, she can be seen climbing walls and jumping from building to building, Citizens of Raven's Pointe have never seen anything like it. Off to Carlos Everett with some of those that saw it happen right before their eyes."

I had a bad habit leaving my T.V on and now I wish I could just kick it off the wall. This wasn't news, but I did it to myself. I was the one that allowed Ryan to turn me into a monster. What I was doing wouldn't be seen as a good deed or helpful. I would turn into another lab rat and be kept quarantined.

"Thanks John, this is Carlos at the scene that some are calling miraculous and some are calling freaky. Here with me I have Tricia. Tricia, what did you see?"

Immediately, I recognized her. It was the woman from last week. I knew this would happen. She sat biting her lip and bouncing from one leg to the other. I didn't care to hear what she was about to say but I couldn't move.

"She's no freak. She saved me the other night. My boyfriend was trying to hurt me and she... she saved me and my son. I never got the chance to tell her thank you. Thank you so much."

My heart expanded, that was what I did it for. I didn't do it because I was bored or because I was superior. I did it to be a helping hand. I owed that to my community. There were so many people that didn't get the justice they deserved or the help they desperately needed. The crooked cops, the crooked mayors, and the crooked politicians didn't care what went in the back alleys, the old buildings that housed those trafficked, it didn't care about the people living off minimum wage or the homeless.

"We have another witness here, your name sir?

"It's Levi, I saw that...that thing hurt that man and then she snapped his neck like it was nothing. The citizens of Raven's Pointe demand justice and demand that this monster be found immediately,"

My heart dropped as I turned the T.V off, the screen went black and I was left staring at my reflection. I wasn't a monster. For all the tough shit I had to do came the good shit. Came the moments that someone was saved from a burning building, a woman saved from an abusive relationship, and kids from becoming sex slaves. That was me, not a monster.

Knock Knock....

The knocking at the door startled and alarmed me. The more they aired the video the more people would catch on and notice it was me. I'm sure it would eventually become obvious by the hair and my attire.

"It's me, Thorn. Let me help you" I heard from the other side of my door.

I didn't know if I could even trust him at this point. I knew a secret about him, but he knew I would never tell. I wasn't built like that, but him, the moment he got in hot grease, he would tell it. Especially, if he gained something from it.

"You can trust me," he said knocking on the door again.

Could I really? I couldn't trust anyone, not even myself. The idea of running from the only home I've ever known had me on the verge of tears. How could I have been so careless?

"You have to let me help you. You can stay at my house in Boloro. I'll keep you safe." He was still pleading with me on the other side of the door. Without thinking, I let him in and fell into his arms. I was weak, stricken with sadness and misery. The tears were flowing, and my heart felt constricted. I was so lost and unsure of myself. For once in my life, I was unsure of my future. Everything in my life had been planned and went according to how I wanted it. This was something I couldn't control, and it was killing me.

"Hey, we gotta move. Grab what you can." He spoke barely above a whisper. It felt good being in his arms again. Feeling him console me the same way he used to, calmed my fears if only for a moment.

Untangling my arms from his torso, I grabbed my bag and anything I felt was important, "We need to get me out of here unseen, any ideas?"

"You the one with the major super powers." He stated with an uneasy chuckle, he was worried for me and that was the little light I needed.

"Pull around to my side of the building," I would have to jump. God this was turning into a major freak show. I couldn't believe that my world had imploded like this.

Leaving out, I waited, and something forced me to turn back on the T.V. and exactly what I knew would happen, happened.

"This just in, we have a name, and a manhunt is being planned at this time for Trulicity McCall. If anyone knows her or her whereabouts, please contact RPPD. We have reports of her being the owner of Tru Findings, CI firm. The phones are going crazy."

These fucking people were acting like this was the Royal Wedding. This was my life. I was waiting on them to release my blood type, social security number and what I ate on my tenth birthday. My photo was being shown and I felt so bad for the backlash my parents were about to receive. That would be my breaking point, fucking with my parents. I wouldn't care about a manhunt; I would destroy this city and expose all its dirty little secrets.

Beep. Beep. It was Thorn beeping the horn. I took one look around my apartment unsure of when I would see it again and sighed. My whole life was here, and the idea of running just didn't seem so strong. I didn't want to leave the life I had made for myself. All my good deeds were being overshadowed. I was never one to run from anything or anyone. And now I had to, and it didn't feel right. But as Thorn continued to beep the horn, I knew I had to if only for a second. Thinking quickly, I started a small fire in my apartment and ran to hit the fire alarm. I couldn't allow them access to my home and files. Everything I didn't have with me would be destroyed. Satisfied with my work as the smoke started to rise and catch on to everything in sight, I ran out the window, I landed directly on my feet.

"That shit is so dope," I heard him say out the car window.

Sliding in the car, we embarked on a journey together again. I devoted so much time to living my life on my terms that I never stopped to think it would catch up to me or cause me this type of strain. I would leave but when I came back I'd be better than ever. They may have had a few images of me but very few got the picture.

Finally Helping Her

Walking into my apartment, I was so glad I didn't have to fight Rose to leave. I knew her well enough that I expected a fight. She wasn't the one to be forced to do anything, but I think she knew her options were limited. We were able to get out of town without incident. They hadn't set up the roadblocks yet but I knew they would be coming.

"Can I get you anything?" I asked. I wanted her to be comfortable. Right now, she was distant, and I understood. She was being labeled as something she wasn't. The fearless woman I loved was full of fear and concern. I felt bad for her and hated that she was in this moment with no relief in sight.

"I just want to be," she responded with a sigh. I understood that as well, sometimes I just sat in my bed with no T.V, no phones on and no one bothering me. I sat until I sorted my thoughts out and was able to think clearly. I would give her that and then we had to get started on clearing her name or at least doing damage control.

"Fa sho, let me at least get you in the shower," I couldn't say how I felt. I felt like I had to help her out of a helpless situation. Once the people said you were one thing, it would take a miracle to get them to see different.

Nodding her head, I grabbed her hand and led her to the shower. She was shaking. I assumed from nerves. Her nerves didn't take away the beauty that was her. I noticed her all those years ago, and the minute I acted on what I noticed it was shattered and stripped away from me without warning. I didn't want that for me and her this time. I never wanted to leave her world. I missed how funny she was, I missed how thoughtful she was, I missed her being my superstar, my number one fan.

"You don't have to do this I have money," she muttered. "I can get myself far away from here," she cried. Wrapping my arms around her, I let her cry until she couldn't cry anymore. I didn't want her to leave or feel like her shit was less important than my shit. We had been down this path before, and this time I wasn't allowing anything to come between what I hoped we were building.

Last week when I finally left her, I couldn't stop thinking of her and how much she had changed. She was a woman unlike any I had ever seen. She went after what she wanted and didn't care who didn't like it. Knowing the shit I faced on a daily basis, made me want the one thing I hated about her, and that was her realness. She didn't sugarcoat shit, and she didn't allow people to fuck over or run over those she loved. I needed that. Erica wasn't going to do that. She would coerce and pressure me to seeing things her way. Not to mention this whole marriage was about her and the scheme she had up her sleeve.

"I'm not afraid of them. I don't even care about the election anymore," I admitted. I didn't, it wasn't what I truly wanted. Watching Cooley high and drinking Smirnoff with her was the wakeup call I needed. I didn't want my life to mirror my father's. He was unhappy, lost in the sauce, and completely detached from who he truly was. That sounded like torture, I didn't want to make a change within myself so grave that it would make me unhappy.

"Don't say that, Dame, you deserve it."

"I do, but not if it means I can't be who I am," I replied. I did deserve to win and have everything I wanted in life. I earned it, but I also deserved true love and to be me. I shouldn't have to marry outside my race to be accepted or to gain the popular vote. I shouldn't have to hide my CD collection or make sure I was prim and proper. I wanted to be the ordinary man that made change, not who they created.

"But it is who you are, you were born for this. I haven't said it but I'm proud of you."

"No, I've been who they've wanted me to be so long," I was starting to feel lightheaded from thinking of what I was about to do, but as she stared at me with those big brown loving eyes. I knew I had to. I had to do this for her and for us. She had me speechless and wrapped around her finger. Which was where I belonged. All that I served to lose could be gained again. "And right now my heart is telling me to do what I need. I'm done living for them."

"Let me take a shower," she whispered. I could feel the need radiating off her as she spoke and dropped her head, and I'm sure she could smell it seeping from my pores. Lust was a hell of a drug. I was yearning for a moment of intimacy with her. I wanted the familiarity I had been missing for a century.

Lighting the candles in the bathroom, I turned her old playlist on. It consisted of Anita Baker, Sade, Lauryn Hill and a little Erykah Badu. She loved neo soul, and truthfully, she turned me on to it also. This was a dark moment and we both needed to feed our souls with each other and good music. As I helped her remove her bra, shirt and jeans, I felt the constriction in my pants. We practically lived together in college but seeing her now was different. Maybe because I was acknowledging my true feeling for her and who she was to me. Rubbing her shoulders to ease the stress of the day, the softness of her skin caused to exhale tightly. She was a magnificent sight. In my head, I was screaming 'hell yea' but I didn't want to jump the gun. I was following her lead.

Reaching in to turn the shower, she kissed me. I could taste the butterscotch on her tongue; this was her favorite candy. Holding her closely, this kiss was something out of a movie. We were hungry for each other and that could be felt from the intensity of the kiss.

Picking her up, I gently sat her on the sink, never breaking the kiss. It was that good. I could kiss her until Jesus returned if I had to. It was clear that we were making up for lost time. But true love never died, and it didn't lie. This was how it was always supposed to be, her being the rose to my thorn. We needed each other more than ever and before I let them take her away from me again, they would have to kill me.

Freeing her breasts, I sucked gently on her long chocolate neck and massaged her breast. She moaned. I almost lost it as she talked back to me. I needed more hands. Two just weren't enough for all that I wanted to accomplish. I had to make up for the time I left her wondering what was good with me. Time that I should have spent waking her up with my head between her legs, time that should have been spent with her legs bent over my shoulder, time that should have been spent fucking her until she was crippled. I wasted time and now I had to make it back and prove myself in the process.

"I've waited so long for you to look at me this way," she admitted, and what was turning into a beautiful moment was over. I backed away, I didn't deserve the most intimate part of her yet. I was honest with myself about not earning it. I hadn't earned it by showing up to keep her safe. It required much more than showing up once. I needed a lifetime to prove that I was worthy.

"I don't deserve this. Let me show you I've changed," I was glad the steam from the shower had clouded her vision of me, it was a sad sight. Hard dick straining to get free. I felt pitiful about how I treated her all those years ago. It wasn't warranted or acceptable. Not only did I hurt her, I hurt my culture. I did exactly what we weren't supposed to and that was turn our back and make our women feel like they weren't worthy of men in high places. It was bullshit, and we needed to fix it and fix it now. I couldn't lie to myself, Rose was and had always been the one for me.

"Not right now, me wanting to just be includes you," she muttered in a cracked voice. This was the go ahead I needed. I still didn't feel like I deserved or earned anything she was willing to give me, but I also wasn't about to turn down this opportunity to make love to my Rose.

I came in closer and our lips met again and from that point shit felt like electricity surging through my body. Her soft callous free hands grazed me as she removed my dress shirt as I tugged at the zipper of her pants we broke our kiss and just stared at each other, she smirked, and it made me smirk.

"Shower sex?" I asked, opening the shower door. My shower hadn't been broken in and I couldn't think of a more fitting time to do so.

"I'd love that,"

Stepping in to the shower, I grabbed her hand and pulled her as she laughed. The water cascaded down her body, and she never looked better. "I love your hair, never change it," I whispered. I loved her hair in its natural state. It didn't matter what I said before, I didn't mean that shit. Her natural curls fit her perfectly, it matched her personality, wild and free. It fucked me up thinking that I had a hand in her wanting to change something so beautiful.

Picking her up, it was easy sliding her down on my man hood, her walls were tight, untouched. I gritted my teeth at the sensation and braced myself by grabbing the shower wall. Her tight walls and my hands gripping her round plump ass was heaven. It was heaven on earth and as I moved her body slow and steady up and down, I saw stars. Everything she did was amazing; it didn't matter what it was. She was the truth at it, completely dedicated to bringing pleasure. I desired to be more like her. She was such a giver.

I turned her around allowing the water to cascade down my back, she arched her back and the curve of her back forced her breast closer to my face. Grabbing one I sucked and pulled lightly, she moaned. That made me go harder. My strokes were deadly and artful, I had a point to prove and I wasn't stopping until I proved that point. Once it was over and done with there would be no question about who was for who; and if my intentions were true.

"Oooo," she moaned and that let me know that this was her spot or maybe she was at her brink, either way I wasn't letting go or slowing down.

"Rose, please forgive me." I sounded like a bitch begging but if this was what I was missing I didn't want to let this moment flee. We needed to address this shit now so tomorrow we could move on as one. Yeah the shit she had between her legs had me ready to romance the shit out of her.

"I forgive you Dame," she screamed as I pounded harder until we both released. It was like we had both just reached the top with no intentions of coming down any time soon. I was singing a tune that had never been sung, 'Shoo do do do do do do doo'.

"Everything I did was wrong, and I'm so sorry. I hope you know it pained me to face each day not being able to see your face or hear your voice," I admitted. After I left, I wondered if she would find someone and if he would appreciate what I didn't. That was some fuck boy shit, but the idea of someone enjoying her wasn't what I wanted, even if I couldn't have her. I wanted to sabotage so much shit but knew I couldn't.

I remembered hearing about her and Khalil through the grapevine and that was the first moment the thorns appeared. I was tripping, and I knew it, but the thought of someone gifting her the life I wanted to give her had me furious. I wondered if I crossed her mind. She was always on mine. I still had one of the many pictures we took in my nightstand. Sometimes I envisioned us cuddled up on the couch watching movies, tickling each other.

"Let's quit talking about it, please?"

"I'm glad you over it but I'm not. I got so much I need to say," I couldn't understand why she kept shutting my apology down. I thought it would bring her some type of joy to hear me admit my wrongs. My ego was feeling bruised. I was ready to apologize and then move past it.

"I don't like words, because anyone can say them. I enjoy action. Show me," she said washing her body and leaving me astonished and amazed. Nothing was left to be said, I would do just as she requested starting tomorrow. I wouldn't have to wonder if I was on her mind. I would make sure I was the first and last thing she thought about.

The next day.......

I woke in five hundred count sheets, naked but not afraid or in a rush. It was a new day. Yesterday happened and it was fresh on my mind, but it wasn't going to stop me. I planned to make some calls check in with my parents and find a way to get my name in the clear.

After last night with Damien, I contemplated just turning myself in again and dealing with whatever they threw my way. If this was going to work, I needed to have the past completely behind me. Loving him in secret wasn't what I wanted. The way he touched my soul last night, the words he spoke to my heart couldn't be hidden. It didn't deserve to be hidden. I had to end this and get it behind me.

"Morning." He spoke bringing me breakfast in bed. It was odd. I knew he was a perfect person who probably hated the thought of me eating in his bed, but I guess this was his chance to show change and say fuck the rules.

"Morning, what's this?"

"Something light. We had a long night," he smiled. After the first round, we went three strong powerful rounds in the bedroom. I had to admit, I didn't think the square before me had a freaky side. I assumed he liked lame as missionary sex. Imagine my surprise when he pulled out handcuffs. The dangerous side of me was jumping for joy, but I played it cool.

"What's on the agenda today?" I asked.

"Nothing major, I need to make some phone calls, but I'm yours all day."

"Are you sure? I can just hang out here," I offered. I couldn't have him stopping his life for me. I appreciated the gesture, but I wasn't that girl anymore. I didn't need him in my face twenty-four seven to feel his love. I was fine with a little space and a little me time. I had to be, for years it was only me. But while I had him and his attention I wouldn't take it for granted.

"Nah, we good. I want to just 'be' right here with you, and the phone calls are for you. I need to pull some strings and get this shit gone," I snickered at him speaking slang. It was so foreign, but it rolled off his tongue effortlessly. The Thorn I knew never cussed. He had such a large vocabulary he saw no need in using a vile word when he could find an eloquent one. I snickered again, looking at his attire. He looked refreshed, in his basketball shorts, no shirt and his corduroy slippers, my nigga even had on a du-rag. "Welcome back, Thorn," I joked.

That made him laugh and tickle me. I was laughing so hard I almost knocked my breakfast to the floor, he knew I was ticklish beyond belief, this was cruel, but I laughed and enjoyed the moment.

"Give it a few days. Hopefully, something else will be the top stories, and I can go back to my regular boring ass life," I advised. I really didn't deserve the attention they were giving to me. I was no one important and I was sure they had more pressing shit to attend do. I was a small fish in a big pond.

"Fuck that, you can't wait around and let them vilify your damn name and brand. You built that shit," his language was turning me on in the worse way. It needed to stop, I was in no shape for an encore of last night.

"I thought we were just being. I don't want to address it right now. I want to eat breakfast, call my parents, and cuddle. Can we just do that and then handle shit tomorrow?" I asked. I really needed a day of nothing, no worries, no conflict and no bullshit. It had been way to long since I had a good day to myself. Between spying on others and saving unappreciative fucks, I hadn't had a real day off in a while.

"Tomorrow, we handle this shit, so we can move on," he presented.

"Deal, what movies do you have?" the way he said we, excited me. The slightest chance of there being a 'we', was like music to ears. Perfect tune, perfect melody on a dope ass hook. It sounded good, it sounded perfect and lovely.

"I'm ashamed to say, that I have like five movies, and all of them are some bullshit," he laughed popping a piece of bacon in his mouth.

"Just show me what you got, I might like it," I'm sure he had nothing that would interest me. As it he made it back with the *American Senator, White House down, and Independence Day*, my thoughts were confirmed. His movie selection was trash and tailored to Damien. Luckily, I brought a few of my own movies; the shit we used to watch as students living off coffee, popcorn and pizza.

"You don't like this?" he asked seemingly offended. I was the one offended at the selection, I asked for movies not a snooze fest. I shook my head no, and watched his eyes soften. I was so focused on the shitty selection he had in his hands I missed the movie behind his back.

"Oh my God you remembered?" I squealed. *Their Eyes Were Watching God* was another one of my favorites. And I couldn't believe he still had my recorded version on VHS, this was a wonderful surprise.

"I watch this movie all the time. The way the Janie feels is how I feel sometimes," I sighed but allowed him to continue, I didn't want to be the person to shut him down or cast his thoughts to the side, "I wanted to be accepted, but now I could care less. I don't care if the color of my skin intimidates them. I just wanted to be whoever I decide at that moment."

"Be you, do you, for you. and if they don't appreciate that fuck 'em'" my slang was always dominant. I code switched from time to time, you know turn on my bill collector voice instead of my ghetto bird voice. Unlike Dame, I mastered being what I wanted to be and being what I knew I needed to be at the same damn time.

"You always know what to say,"

Kissing my nose, we moved the breakfast tray and snuggled under the covers as the movie took us to another place. As we watched, the time felt like the present. A woman forced by her family to marry for status. He's older, she's uneducated, but a lover and full of romance and questions. Loved for her beauty and obedience and not her mind, she finally finds love with my man named Tea Cake. Finally, love takes the place of stability, only for him to die from fucking rabies. It was truly tragic, and as I watched, the tears pooled in my eyes at the same scene that literally takes my breath away.

"I can't believe I still cry from this movie."

"I can, it's a hard reality and many don't even know that they are living in it, including me."

"Well you don't have to anymore; we can have it all." I sounded weak and feeble and before I could change my mind or my tone. He kissed me taking the air right from my lungs. There was a God with his eyes on us, and my eyes were on him.

***

"Are you and Carlos still friends?" I asked. He would be my inside scoop and the solution to my problem if only momentarily. Carlos worked with the news station and although he was a complete creep he would look out for his best friend.

"Yeah, why what's up?"

We laid naked in bed with pizza boxes covering the bed and the boring ass movies he had playing in the background. He sat up and looked me in my eyes. My wheels were turning, and I had all I needed to hopefully create the diversion we were waiting for.

"I need him to release the conversation between Erica and Ryan. I also have pictures to prove it." I breathed, glad I had a second to think and forget about the trouble knocking at my door.

"You got it with you?" he asked.

"I grabbed what I could before I torched the apartment." I knew all my work would come in handy. This would be the perfect angle. It would not only take the attention off me but buy Damien some time to with the election.

"I'll call him over," he said grabbing for his phone. He made the call while I grabbed my laptop and pulled up the recorded conversation. I also had a feeling that I should listen to see if she had been speaking of anything else.

Pressing play, her voice played over my laptop loudly and clearly. This conversation was from yesterday.

"Ryan what the fuck are we going to do now?" she asked.

"Erica, you need to chill. I've got people going to her home now."

She huffed and puffed not satisfied with his answer and they were both in for a surprise when they realized there was no home to go to. Damien and I sat silently listening to the recording waiting for her to say more incriminating shit. This was getting better by the day.

"That won't matter, she can't be seen in public her face is all over the damn news. That video has went viral. This is a fucking mess." She fussed.

"Rose is very resourceful, you'd be surprised at what she can do. Go have a drink, spend your father's money or something I have it handled."

"I'm calling it off, we wait until he wins and then just eliminate him." She *suggested.*

"Do you really want blood on your hands Erica? You need to speak with your father about that." Ryan reasoned.

"Father won't understand, he doesn't want him to win but our reasons aren't the same. And I don't care about blood on my hands if I get to live the life I want, make it happen or your payments stop."

Looking over at him he seemed shocked. I on the other hand wasn't. I knew something was off with her from the beginning. I hated it for him because I'm sure he had some level of love and mutual respect for her, but the truth would soon reveal itself and he needed to be thankful that it came before his body was lowered in the ground.

"Carlos will be hear soon, what else do you have?" he asked.

"Pictures and recordings. Can we trust him?" I asked. It had been awhile since I seen or heard from Carlos. I knew him to funny and carefree, but I also knew that once the SSRP got their fangs in you, you felt indebted. I would hate to trust him with the only thing that could help me clear my name and him turn on me.

"Los is straight. He was always rooting for us. I'm sure now it would be no different now."

Feeling a little relieved, I finished burning the recordings to a CD. My spirits were lifting with the hope of being able to live a normal life again. I would take a break no more cases for a while. I would be a recluse, because this wouldn't remove the video or the ideas that people had of me. This would only make the bigger fish back off.

The door bell ringing alerted us that we had a visitor. Throwing on our clothes quickly Thorn went and answered the door, and I heard his big mouth before I seen him. His larger than life personality hadn't changed. Carlos was one of the only people that could bring Thorn out without much effort.

"Tell me something good, it sounded serious over the phone." He said giving Thorn dap. I rounded the corner and heard, "Damn bro, for real?"

Smiling I embraced Carlos, it had been a long time and he was still a big 6'5 teddy bear that had a joke about everything. "Hey los, can you help a sista out?"

"Man, anything for you, tell me what I can do?" he asked. Sizing me up, I wondered how they remained friends for so long. Carlos was a womanizer and he didn't care to tell it.

"You covered the story about me and I need you to cover another one. But this one is about Erica. Can you do that?" I asked. I really wasn't going to take No for an answer. I had to twist his arm literally to get him to do what we needed but I wasn't against it. I would be the monster they were really painting me to be if it meant I got out of this shit.

"What's the story?" he asked.

Without answering, I played the recording of Erica and Ryan's communication. I needed him to understand the severity and sensitivity of what I was asking. This would up his ratings and ensure that it got out to the right people. I couldn't mail or take it myself and wait for someone to intercept. It had to be done and it had to be done tomorrow.

"Damn, that's what you do now?" he asked.

"Yea, that's what I've always done. I just had to be slick because something wasn't right about her. Can you help?"

"I can help but they are out for blood. It's been a big ass mess at the station. I'm sure I can switch the story and expose the shit that's going on. I need a favor though." He rubbed his hands together looking sneaky.

"What?" I asked, rolling my eyes. Someone always wanted something for something. It was annoying, but I would hear his request and see what I could do.

"I want Colleen. Make that happen for ya', boy and I got you." He smiled.

"Colleen is mean, and you will not be able to handle her like a common slut." I laughed.

"I can tame her snow bunny ass, just hook it up," he responded. Writing her number down on a piece of paper, I slid it over. This was an easy favor. She was always trying to play matchmaker for me and now I had the chance to do it for her. Carlos and her would be a disaster, but that wasn't my concern. She said she was ready to settle down, hopefully Carlos was also.

"Call her and let her know I'm safe please." I asked.

Carlos left and now we played the waiting game. I prayed that this worked and bought me some time to get shit situated or get further from town. I would have to go to the other side of Avia to be safe. That wasn't what I wanted but if this didn't work I wouldn't be left with a choice. I knew this was God's plan hence the reason I was being stretched and challenged. I knew he wouldn't leave me in a state of unrest. I had to get on my knees and pray for safety and that his will be done.

"Let's get some sleep." Thorn said making sure the doors were locked and that we were back to safety in his bedroom. Never in a million years did I think our pride would be put to the side and we would once again be a team.

"You thought it would be easy to run from me?" Ryan said in a chilling tone. I rubbed my eyes hoping his vision would fade, but the more I rubbed the angrier his face became. I didn't understand what he was getting at. I didn't plan this; I didn't facilitate this shit on purpose.

"What?" I asked attempting to make sense of what he was getting at. The closer he got the more I became worried. How did he find me and where was Damien? I prayed he hadn't set me up or left me to the hands of the same man that created me.

"Tru, you owe me. I created you and I plan to destroy you before you can destroy me," his laugh was menacing and dark. I attempted to get up, but my body felt like it was made of a ton of bricks. My vision was getting hazy, my eyes so heavy, my body misty from sweat.

"Help," I screamed, "Help" my screams were falling on deaf ears. No one was coming to my rescue and the walls were closing in. My breathing became labored as panic set in. The last few days had been exactly what I needed. Time to detach from the world and decide what I wanted to. I couldn't let Ryan take me without putting up a fight. He would turn me in and act like he knew nothing of what he did to me, to us. Now that my bubble had burst about being the only one, I was sure there were more of us stupid enough to allow him to alter our state.

"Dame," I screamed. It was like it used to be. Me searching for him and waiting for him to save me. "Dame, I need you," I needed him to for once come save me. I needed him to finally acknowledge how important I was and that it was my turn to have his love and dedication.

"He can't save you; he could never save you." Ryan mocked while I attempted to gain enough strength. "Rose, you are nothing and Damien knows that. It was all staged."

I felt the veins in my arm tingle and the strength come. I was going to shut Ryan up one way or another. I couldn't allow him to think he had won. I was more than some super natural freak he created. I was more than a science project. As my strength came back, Ryan began to fade.

"Rose, Rose," I heard Dame say as he shook me. Eyes popping open, it was all a dream. I looked around in a state of confusion. I was still at his apartment and Ryan wasn't in sight.

"It was a set up," I said jumping out of bed searching for my clothes. I needed to go pay Ryan a visit. I knew he was expecting me, and I always delivered. I wasn't safe either way. I would find my way to death. It would take an army to kill me and they had better get it ready.

"Chill." He spoke calmly. Too calmly if you asked me. We were being hunted, and he was telling me to chill. As I searched for my bag, I stopped and focused on Dame. I couldn't tell if he was moving funny or not. He was dressed in his normal suit and tie. He was opening the blinds and acting as if my dream didn't happen. It felt so tangible. I saw Ryan, and I heard him loud and clearly.

"Are you setting me up?" I asked. I needed to know if this was all a hoax, a ploy to get ahead. It wouldn't be the first time he fucked me over for his own personal gain. But the way we touched, the secrets we shared and the love that was made. It would make it so hard to kill him, but I would. I would fuck him up and not apologize for it. He was out of chances to fuck me over. I lived my whole life repairing myself from the bullshit he did to me. I wouldn't go so easily this time. This time he would know I was there and that I wasn't for his games.

"Why would I do that?" he asked offended. It was frustrating me that I couldn't read him. I couldn't tell if he was lying, fronting, or truly giving us a shot.

"I had a dream. Ryan said he set me up," It sounded crazy, but the subconscious mind wasn't so fucking far. It made sense to me. Ryan probably got wind of me and Damien from that fucking Khalil. He was a piece of work and it wouldn't surprise me if he had him tailing me.

191

"Why would he do that?" he asked, like he didn't know that Ryan was never one to be trusted. He would smile in your face and be the main one taking the stand and whispering with his buddies.

"I think he had someone, well, Khalil following me." I had never been caught up the way I was the other day. Granted, a few people had seen me in action but never enough to identify and point me out.

"Khalil from college? The one that always had a thing for you." He smirked.

"This isn't the time for fucking egos," he didn't want to go there with me. Khalil wasn't shit but at least he didn't think I was to ethnic for him. He gave me the time of day, he was smart, he was handsome, he would've been perfect if I liked men that hadn't allowed their balls to drop.

"I'm just saying, I heard that was your boo for a moment."

"What does that have to do with anything?" I asked he was naïve if he thought I couldn't and didn't deserve a life after him. "Khalil was a fling, but that doesn't have a damn thing to do with him following me. Stay focused."

"Ok, your dream, what did Ryan say?"

I didn't want to repeat what was said. The more I repeated it and put it out to the atmosphere the easier it would be to become true. The love was flowing through my veins. If he was being straight up with me, I wouldn't allow the universe to take it away from me again.

"He set me up. The day everything went down was no different than any other day, but somehow people came out of nowhere. I've never been able to be identified. I've been saving and helping the people of Ravens Pointe for years."

"Did it feel different?"

"Yeah, I felt it, but couldn't turn my back on helping that mother. Now I wonder if it was staged." Flopping down on the bed, I felt stupid and realized that I had been finessed. My emotions were played on and it could cost me my life. Ryan sent Khalil because he knew it would frustrate me and knock me off my square.

"Don't worry, I'm ending it today. That's why I'm dressed. I have a press conference." I had no clue what he planned to do, and although I got the warm fuzzies from his statement, I couldn't let him place himself in the line of fire.

"No, Da-" my words were cut off by a kiss, a full-on open mouth almost sensual kiss. I saw fireworks and tingled with desire. Before I could gather my thoughts and protest, he pulled away and left me standing there to wonder what happened and what it was all about.

Sitting on the edge of the bed, my emotions were blazing my insides. I went years without feeling anything. No love, no sadness, and no adversity, well not of my own. All my sensitivity come from my love of other people. But now, now that Damien was back and allowing his love to pour out. I felt the burden that he was attempting to save himself from all those years ago. He wanted to save me but now I needed to save him. I loved Damien, I'm talking that get out of bed in the morning and he's the first thing I think about. I mean that love that has you smiling with nothing to smile about, the love that provided a home within them. I loved the mess we created, I loved the compassion and the selflessness we were now crossing over to.

Attempting to focus on something else, I turned on the news. I had been waiting all morning to hear from Carlos about the secrets airing but nothing, until I seen his bald head come on the screen.

"Avia, we've had a pretty interesting week, the other day we had a false reporting of a superhero terrorizing the streets and today, today we have some piping hot tea to share with you about Avia's prominent family the Wainwrights.

We allow people here to think they can do whatever and get away with it depending on the money they have, but today, that stops. This is a serious moment, and I need you all to listen and focus.

An anonymous recording came in last night about Erica Wainwright, the pictures you are seeing on your screen deserve your attention as she is clearly cozy with some unknown woman. Are we going to allow those that make the rules break them? Are we going to crucify a good Samaritan instead of paying attention to what we have before us. An adulterer and a murderer. After the commercial, we get deep into the things that are going on with the Wainwright family. Stay tuned."

Dialing my mother, I needed to say what needed to be said. I wasn't sure what the outcome would be when I surrendered but I need my family to know that I loved them tremendously and was so thankful that I had them on my side and in my corner.

"Ma," I said as she answered the phone with a solemn voice.

"Rose," she whispered. It was ten o'clock in the morning I was sure she was at work. My mother was a dispatcher for this police department. She had done this job for many years and I knew my love for saving people came from her.

"Are you at work?" I asked.

"Barely, my body's here, but not my mind," she replied. I knew that meant they had got to her and she was worried sick about me and if I would be ok.

"Don't worry, mom, it's almost over." I muffled a cry because I had no idea of the outcome. I didn't know if I would ever be able to see or hear from them again. I didn't know if this would work or if they

194

would kill me on sight. This wasn't the shit I thought about when I agreed. I knew this wouldn't stay a secret forever, but I thought it would be my truth to reveal when I was ready.

"Why didn't you tell me, baby?"

"Tell you what? That I allowed some man to make me a mutant, or that I save people that are now against me." I couldn't tell her what I did. She would have had so many foul words for me. I was headstrong and that was a weak decision I made to get back at Damien. But she couldn't be told that, she loved Damien and she worshipped his parents up until the other day. I would be completely upset if she took his side over mine.

"I'm your mother, Rose. I raised you, and I know when something is up. You never been a good liar, I knew."

"That's not important right now, I just wanted to call and let you know how much I loved you. I mean, I really love you, Momma. I thank you for being such a strong woman and someone I could look up to. I prayed that one day I'd be able to give my kids that same love and strength, tell daddy, I love him too. Now I doubt I get that chance but I'm ok with that, these are the cards I've been dealt."

"The Rose I raised doesn't accept defeat. Fight," she said disconnecting.

I didn't have the fight in me, it was like my powers were retreating. I just wanted to save Damien from ruining his life because I ruined mine. Both of us didn't need to be captured and God knows what else. This was my situation and I needed to handle it alone.

Grabbing a pen and paper, I wrote Damien a letter.

Thorn,

I remember the first day I actually fell in love with you. I've tried to forget it, but how could I? It was magical, almost unreal. I still remember that day because it was a day that changed my

195

life. I was annoyed, but that smile, and your persistence stuck with me. No one had ever smiled at me with such joy, other than my father. I fell in love that day and I was so happy when we became attached at the hip. If Thorn was there, Rose would be there also. That's when we affectionately donned the phrase 'rose to my thorn'. It was so true. There was no me without you.

When shit went left, I hated you. I hated that you couldn't and wouldn't see me the way I saw you. I hated that you over looked me knowing I was and would always be the one that completed you.

I forgive you, I truly do. I can only imagine how difficult it was for you to have to say goodbye to the one friend that knew you for you and loved you for you no matter what.

I've shut you down this entire time because I just didn't want to take the time we had with each other for granted. We had so much making up to do. We had so much love to make up for. I didn't want that to be overshadowed by sadness and flared tempers.

Now I wish we would have just stayed apart to begin with. What I plan to do isn't easy but its needed. I can't let you ruin your life because of me. I told you that I didn't want your apologies, and I meant that. I want you to succeed. I want you to have what you deserve, and that's a chance at making the world a better place. I want us parting many years ago to be worth it.

It was hell not having you around for the silliest shit, let's not make that be in vain.

Love Always, Rose

P.S you will always be the thorn to my rose!

Sealing the envelop, I changed into all black attire. My black boots, black tank top and black leggings. I braided my hair back into the two braids. I decided to leave my favorite jacket for Dame. I left my phone, and all my belongings. I didn't need any of it where I was going. This could be considered some form of suicide, but it didn't matter at this point. My mind was made up and this was the right thing to do.

"I love you, Dame."

Stepping out the door and starting my journey, the streets were empty. I was surprised. I just knew people with pitchforks and torches would be littering the streets on the search for me. The reward was increasing by the day and who didn't love free money? It was odd, but I pressed on. Jumping from building to building would be the quickest way for me to make it to Raven's Pointe. The quest for freedom was on.

Today I Choose You

A thorn defends the rose harming only those who would steal the blossom-
Chinese Proverbs

Stepping from my car, I took a deep breath and prayed about the sacrifice I was making for not only Rose but for myself. I knew she would try and stop me if she knew I was resigning and pulling myself from the race. I kissed her one last time because things would change after I told everyone what was going on. Still, I proceeded. It was now or never with me. I had to do this in order to live my life on my terms.

"Don't do this." My publicist was hell bent on cancelling this press conference. I couldn't be persuaded. I appreciate all he had done for me, but it would take god himself coming down to tell me not to take this chance.

"It's been a good run, but I'm done," I was finished with this masquerade and it had nothing to do with Rose. I wanted this for me. Only thing she did was remind me of what life could be like with her. I wanted her, and I couldn't have that if I continued with the race. This was the best way to save her from herself.

"Dame, it's been a pleasure," Ivan always wished me well and I was sad that all our hard work would be a waste but fuck it. It was time to live and that's exactly what I planned to do.

"Same, here" I replied with a shake of the hand. It was now or never. Play time was over with. Over the last few days, I had been working endlessly to set up a press conference without her knowledge. It was difficult because we had been stuck like glue the entire time she was at my home, I loved it, but I couldn't get anything done watching her silky-smooth skin prance around my place, I got a chill thinking about her.

"There's still time for us to come up with something else," he said giving it one more shot.

"No, we do it now, don't mention it again," I said a little forceful. My point clearly wasn't getting across if he kept attempting to change my mind. This press conference would serve for many purposes me to pass the torch and secondly to expose Ryan and Erica. By now the news had hit the airways and I could flip and play the victim of conspiracy to commit murder. I had no doubt in my mind that this would be a problematic task. He wasn't one to back down or accept blame but he wouldn't be able to deny my abilities also.

Walking up to the podium, I peered out into the sea of Raven Pointe natives. I loved my people but after what happened with Rose, I knew they didn't love me back. Awful shit was being said about her and they didn't even know her. They knew what the media wanted them to know. They didn't know how loving and understanding she was. They didn't know that the thorn in her side was also her rose. She loved helping others. It had always been like that. They didn't know that she was her parents' pride and joy. And they didn't know that I, the next senator was madly in love with her.

I could hear the crowd cheering for me as I stepped up the podium. It was pandemonium. The cheers were ear splitting and for just a second, I considered changing my mind, but I knew my stretch of being someone I wasn't had reached the end. Tapping the mic and clearing my throat, I waited for the crowd to simmer down.

"Afternoon citizens of Raven's Pointe," before I could continue, the crowd roared again and I was left smiling and waiting for this shit to be over. The quicker I called this election off, the quicker me and Rose could skip town and lay low. It was a risk I was willing to take. I wanted us to be away and start over. We couldn't continue to waste time with love.

"I'm here today, to discuss a few things that have been going on in our community. I know we would all love to live in a perfect world but that's impossible. Raven's Pointe isn't perfect and with the latest news circulating about the PI, I'm saddened by how easy it was for us as citizens and humans to condemn a woman we don't even know." I paused gathering my thoughts for the next statement. "Trulicity Rose McCall, is a super. She's not a monster. She's not a criminal. She does not need or deserve to be locked away and shunned for a wild night of experimentation. I've known this woman since we were still trying to figure out our life. It was college that she allowed me to be her study buddy. Yes, she attended an Ivy League school, same as me and some of you. This is the same woman that years ago became the rose to my thorn. This same woman has been more than a family friend to me.

I am here today to let you all know that if capturing her is what you want to do that's fine, but I will not stand idly by and watch. Tru has used her powers for good and all it took was one bad day to exonerate all that. The cliché saving babies from burning buildings, helping victims of abuse escape their captors, all of that has taken place and made Raven's Pointe a safer place. She's done things that your own police couldn't and wouldn't do. That should count for something.

I honestly wish I had the strength and the willpower to be who she is and do what she has done without request. Some of us get the freedom of being able to turn our cheeks to those in need, she doesn't. It's now in her DNA to save and rescue those that can't fend for themselves.

I recommend that this hunt be called off and stopped immediately. Furthermore, I remove my name from-"

"Noooo," I heard her scream from far off in the distance before I could finish my well thought out planned speech. "Dame don't do this, please." she said as the crowd started to disperse and part for her to make it to the podium.

"Rose, what are you doing? They will kill you, and I can't let that happen," I said stepping down from the podium. After finally receiving the best love I ever had, I couldn't let them harm her and ultimately remove her again from my life. She had always been in my heart and in my thoughts. But having her back opened my eyes to all I was missing. All that I could miss for the rest of my life.

"I don't care anymore, you and I both know you won't be happy doing this," she reasoned.

"It's too late, I've made my mind up," I spoke. We were at eye level and speaking like only lovers do. "Rose, I should have stuck up for you years ago, I refuse to leave you all by yourself again. This ain't me." I spoke with her hands in mine.

"This isn't your sacrifice." She whispered. Her point was invalid to me, success didn't equate happiness for me anymore. It was love that I desired, and the rest would fall into place. Erica wasn't important anymore, saving face for my family wasn't important anymore and saving this town wasn't important if she wasn't able to be by my side.

"This is for the sake of you and me, and you have the right to feel how you feel, but turning a blind eye would still have me living for them, and if I'm going to live for anyone, it's going to be you."

As we stared each other down, waiting for one to break and give in, the transformation began to take ahold of me. From the corner of my eye I could see the police led by Ryan approaching.

"Ahh, imagine finding you two love birds together attempting to save one another." Ryan smirked. Not breaking contact, I could see the transformation taking place within her as well. Things were about to get out of control and at this point all we had was each other. Turning our backs to one another we prepared for a battle. We were outnumbered by the police. Hell, we were surrounded.

"Why would you set me up? I've always done everything you and that damn society has asked for." She asked.

"Rose, you really think you can cross me and get away with it?"

"You crossed me, you think I don't know you set all this shit up?" she asked.

"Rose, you owe me, simple." I was raging inside, ready and prepared to rip Ryan to shreds as he continued to calmly speak like all this wasn't his fault.

"Rose don't listen to him you don't owe him shit." I spoke through gritted teeth. Ryan was a no worse than a low-level scam artist. Promises for this and that when all the while everything he did was attached to something else. I wished she wouldn't have shown up. He knew she would be here to stop me once she found out. This was another set up. But I would die today saving her.

Ryan

Watching Damien whine and moan like a bitch on stage was comical. It was cute but wouldn't spare him or Rose from the treachery. I wanted this all to end. Damien made the ultimate mistake of coming to the rescue. I wouldn't hesitate to kill them both, when I only really wanted Rose.

"It was all a setup, kill two birds with one stone." I whispered in her ear before sticking a needle in Tru's neck. Instantly she fell in my arms. "Carry her away," I ordered. Watching her red hue leave, I knew the serum worked. I was no fool, I knew I nor the police would be no match for Tru. I knew the power she possessed and what I gifted her with. Over the years her powers had increased way beyond my belief.

Each time she came to be tested, we realized something new she had. When I picked her, I had no idea it would take the way it had. She was all powerful. There were no limits to what she could train herself to do.

"Why did you pick Tru?" Khalil asked as we watched her through the one-way mirror. Two weeks had passed since my initial test and today it was a joy to watch her use the powers I gave her. I felt extremely accomplished and I knew it would only go up from here. Tru was the first subject for my experiment, and so far, things were looking promising. Soon I would go down as the best scientist in the world. If I had the ability to alter DNA and change a human to a beast I could do anything. This would put me in the top tier with the society.

"Vulnerability and anger," Science wasn't all about lab rats and sterile rooms, a person had to want it as bad as I wanted to give it to them. Secretly, I watched the change with Tru and Damien. The dynamic changed making Tru vulnerable and almost desperate for change. I played the shadows, watching her change her wardrobe, her hair and even how she responded to her peers. She was defenseless and willing to do anything to remove the feeling of not being good enough for him or anyone else. "I simply wanted to give her something else to do with her time other than worry about Thorn." I responded.

I could have come to Tru and told her that I could make her a white woman, and for Thorn, she would have done it without question. I saved her from herself. I knew that doing this would be a beautiful powerful distraction from the self-hate she was living in. She would be powerful, strong and a rarity. She would be like no other.

"She's beautiful, did you give her powers to love me?" he asked. I chuckled. Khalil would never be on the level of Rose. Khalil rode the fence, he talked a good game, but no one could deny Tru's strength without the powers. She fell victim to Dame and his mind games but no one else would ever get that from her. She wouldn't be fooled twice or easily persuaded to love again. Khalil didn't stand a real chance.

"My friend, I'm afraid you'll have to do that on your own."

I continued to watch her, proud of myself for reading her correctly. It was a personal decision to use Tru, I knew she would feel indebted to me. I knew she would appreciate what I gifted her with. At first, it didn't seem like much of a gift with the vomiting, cold sweats and feeling of death but now she was a animal. Her anger was already present, but the serum made her go harder.

"That's good, Tru, come see me in the office." I spoke over the intercom. It normally took fifteen minutes for her to come down and I had to let her do that or be caught in the crossfire of her rage. The first few days I had to get her locked to her bed and in her room. We had several situations, that left some injured and others just walked out refusing to be a part of her shit anymore.

"Ryan, my wounds are healing instantly. Was that apart of this?" she asked. Other than super strength none of the things we had figured out were a part of it, but with science it was a lot of trial and error. This was just one of the things I was learning about the genes I used on her.

"Tru, let me be honest with you, there's a lot of things that may happen or change over time. That's just science. I can't say everything that will happen."

"Ryan, the minute I think I have something under control or figured out, something else comes out the wood work and scares me and the people around me." *She fussed.*

I was concerned, but we couldn't turn back now. We would just have to ride the wave. It was never my intention to make her all powerful or indestructible but again I had no idea what all the serum would to do her, it worked differently from subject to subject.

"I understand, but we will just have to keep an eye on it and practice control."

That was the only moment I felt that I may have made a mistake and moved to quickly. Tru was the most powerful subject I had to date. Anybody that came after her, had a watered down and tailored serum. I wanted super humans but not any that had the ability to take over the world.

"Thorn, nice message." I laughed turning to leave. He would never have more clout than me. I ran the secret society and everything he said to the people would hold no value as to what I could do. What I would do next. Tru would be locked away and Thorn had just stuck the last nail in the coffin. Raven Pointe's newest senator would win the election by a land slide and Erica would be free to live her own miserable life, and I'd be richer than my wildest dreams. "I win, Thorn. Like always."

That woman and her baby weren't in danger, I framed Tru. I knew she would never find anything on Damien he was perfect and the perfect candidate. He was the most dangerous candidate. No secrets meant he could turn the ideas of Raven Pointe upside down. No scandals meant that people would trust him and start to question the very foundation we stood on. Damien had walked the straight line to the point that the other candidate didn't stand a chance. It was a no brainer for the town to elect Damien. His work spoke for itself.

"Ryan, cut the bullshit," he said. Thorn was so foolish. My plan had worked perfectly. I got them back together and the love sparked between them. I knew it would be easy to get her on his side, and then I would strike on her. Which would leave him wanting to change history and him to get in front of the town and withdraw his bid for the senator. The plan worked perfectly, causing me to smile. Sometimes I didn't know I had it in me until everything worked out with no hiccups.

"All it took was you and Tru to get in the same room, and that stupid love-sick shit would start all over. I knew from the minute your file came across my desk it would be her to bring you down without trying." I shrugged. I was a maniac, a true mad scientist. I swindled and slithered my way through life and this was why without super powers I was the powerful one. My mind was no match for love. It made people mindless and desperate. So desperate that I got everything I wanted without lifting a finger. I played the puppet master, I sailed the ship.

"That's just it, Ryan, I haven't been brought down. Have I?" he asked, staring into my eyes. It was an uncomfortable stare. I couldn't tear my eyes from his, it was like he had mind control over me. "Ryan didn't win, did he?" he asked the crowd. "Ryan didn't win" the crowd repeated. Everyone was standing still, no blinking, and only listening to everything he said and commanded them to do.

"No, no you haven't," I replied. His stare was still blank and menacing. I wanted to look away, but it was impossible. My mind was blank. His eyes were completely black in color. I felt like I was staring right into the devil's eyes, but the only image that could be seen was my own reflection.

"Good, I knew you would say that. Now tell the police that everything is ok and to leave." He ordered.

"Leave, everything is ok here," I repeated. The officers dropped Tru. He grabbed my neck, lifting me from the ground. And tossed me into the crowd. I watched as he helped Tru up from the ground. She was weak, but the red hue was coming back to her skin. It didn't make sense, that cocktail should have had her out for hours.

"Everything you touch is tainted," she said with a feeble voice attempting to stand up on her own. "You are constantly ruining lives because you have the power. And instead of using it for the greater good you constantly use it for evil. How selfish can you be? People are sick and in need of help and you would rather treat them like pawns. You deserve death, you are a waste."

"Tru, I made you, without me you would still be crying over Thorn," I smirked. She forgot I was there with her when she was at her lowest. The secret dreams she had of marrying Thorn, the calling out for him in the middle of the night, or the fact that this was all because of him. "You would still be weak and hanging onto someone who never saw your worth in the first place. I saw your worth I knew you could be great. He's the one you should kill." I screamed. I was willing to say and do anything I could to save myself. I had no idea Thorn possessed the power to control minds.

"Ryan, there's still time for you to make this right. You've got one chance. Get up."

"Tell me what you need me to do." I asked. I would figure the rest out from there, but I had to save myself. For years I had the power to skate away from my faulty practice, my lies, and my bullshit but I didn't see the end coming from this one. Damien and Tru had me exactly where they wanted me. I had no out or fight in this anymore. Sadly, I didn't even care any longer. I was ready to live a normal life the way I wanted it and that's what I would do if I made it out of this situation with my life.

"The truth. It's that simple. Clear her name." he spoke kneeling in front of me. Everything seemed to have calmed down, but the crowd was still under his control. Standing to my feet I dusted myself off.

"Walk to the podium," he instructed, and I made my way to the podium. Once I did this, I would be the one on the chopping block not them. The Wainwrights, my parents and the society would all be after me or disown me.

"Then what?" I asked. The closer I got to the podium the more I thought about the aftershock and the amount of damage control that would have to be done.

"Tell them what you've done." He instructed. I did as I was told. The crowd was still in a daze. But Damien came closer and stood off to the side with Tru now right next to me.

"Roll the cameras." He spoke into the mic. On cue the cameras were back rolling. I had an empty feeling in the pit of my stomach. My mind was drifting to the worse possible scenario. I wanted to just flee the scene, but I had nowhere to go and no easy way to get there. This was happening whether I wanted it to or not. It was best to just get it over with.

"Look at the camera and tell the people Rose was set up."

"Rose was set up." I repeated looking into the eyes of those in attendance. Everyone seemed to be back to normal but me.

"Tell them she is not a monster and it was self-defense," he whispered.

"She is not a monster, she was only acting out of self-defense." You would have thought he had a gun to my head with how easy it was for me to repeat and obey. He was in charge and my puppet master ways where gone.

"Tell them all about what you've done. Tell them who you are." He whispered.

"My name is Ryan Scott, and I have to tell you all what I've done to tear families and people apart. The city officials pay me a lot of me to help them get their way and get who they want on their side. I set Rose up and was paid by the Wainwrights to make him lose this election." I spoke, it seemed fairly more of my own thoughts than those directed by Thorn. I looked back and his eyes were back to their original state. No longer dark and commanding. I contemplated stopping this charade and taking my chances, but I also knew that I would be taking a major risk.

"I thought for a long time that I could get away with my shortcomings but as you see they've caught up to me," I briefly laughed. "I apologize for ruining so many lives with my childish actions. Rose has been a good friend of mine for years and so has Damien, and it pains me that I've stooped so low and caused so much trouble. He is the best candidate you will ever see for Senate. Please forgive me for this entire mix up and for the trouble I have caused." I stepped down and started for my car. The crowd was booing me and shoving me as I made my way through. This was the least of my concern. I knew my phone would be blowing up and my face and name would be the talk of our small town. I let a lot of people down, however I was feeling free.

Pulling out my phone, I called the last person I thought I would ever call, my sister colleen, *"Hey sis, I'm leaving town in a few. I know our relationship has been non-existent for some time, but I wanted to say I love you."*

"Ryan, I'm so proud of you, and I appreciate you for saving my friend."

Disconnecting the call, I started my car and planned to drive until I found myself in a new area completely starting over. No turning back and no worrying about the backlash I would receive.

It Worked

"Oh, my God, I can't believe he did that without fucking it up." I said ecstatic that I was in the clear. Damien's word wouldn't have been good enough. Although I appreciated his effort. Lord knows it meant the world to me to finally see him sticking up for but even more for what was right.

"We can get married now," he replied.

I gasped and whipped my neck way to hard thinking I heard him mistakenly. *Did he say we could get married?* I asked myself. Marriage was a big step and sure it had always been my dream but was it right. My mouth was wide open and the small flutters in my belly returned. I felt like that meant it was right. Nervousness normally sent me in to fight or flight mode, but I was neither. My feet were planted on what seemed like solid ground and my heart was extending to his.

"Thorn, what?" I asked. Before amazement and all the excitement took over I needed to make sure I heard him correctly. My dream of marrying my best friend of so many years dated back to the first time I actually laid eyes on him and if this was going to happen I needed him to be sure this was exactly what he wanted.

"Now that you are in the clear, and I don't have anyone holding me back, we can get back to you being the rose to my thorn. It's long overdue and I can't think of anything that would make my life complete than finally being with you for real. Think about it," he said kissing my forehead.

"Don't do this out of obligation. You know I hate that shit." I replied. I didn't want him to feel that he had to do this because of how fucked up things left off in the past. It was the past and now that the elephant was no longer in the room friends would be acceptable to me. I still wanted success for him with or without me. And it was no longer personal if he couldn't have them with me, especially after this situation.

"I'm only obligated to not fucking myself over again when it comes to you. I let you go once, and I won't do it again."

"Ok, let me get this over with," I responded.

I felt compelled to address the crowd. I knew Ryan gave his version of the things that went on, but it was watered down to me. I wanted to speak for myself on behalf of myself. No one would be able to tell the story better than me.

"Attention Attention," I spoke. There weren't very many still in attendance, but I wanted to just say a quick word. "My name is Trulicity and I wish I had something grand to say about the recent events, but I don't. I am who you see, a black woman with the heart to save. You can all judge me and persecute me for being that, but it won't change my need and desire to save those that need it the most. Constantly we turn a blind eye to those that need our help simply because they are different than us. What would a world look like if we lend a hand without expecting anything in return? It would look like ME! You all attempted to throw rocks and ruin me, but you only activated my oil. I am better, I am wiser, but mostly importantly I am free."

I stepped down from the podium into the arms of the last person I figured would have my back. My shoulders were square, I was back and done carrying the grief of what I used to be. I was relieved of the baggage I carried silently for years. I had been fighting to take breaths for years they were effortless right now.

"I love you, Thorn," I said into his chest. This was worth the sacrifice. This was worth the risk. Finally, he felt the same, it was more than about politics, safety this was all about emancipation and getting exactly what you deserved, what you earned.

212

"I love you too Rose, let's get out of here before everyone changes their mind." He joked.

Briefly the worlds idea or judgements crossed my mind, but I didn't let it dawdle. We would address the worlds opinion when it became pertinent. We would address his mother when it became necessary. Right now, I only wanted to address the time passed between us. There was so much we need to relish in and I was more than prepared to take the time to learn all the things of Thorn that I didn't know I needed to understand.

I couldn't take his drive and dedication personal, because truthfully my drive matched his. Our passions were the only difference. If he was willing I was willing. Nothing stood in our way now, we were free to love and explore the many possibilities of our future.

I lied to myself for years, I pretended that if he came back asking for another chance that I wouldn't give it. But I would that's how strong, exuberant, and true our love was. It dared not dwindle from years elapsed. We were connected to one another like ancient history. Our dirty, grimy faces and tattered clothes couldn't diminish the beauty of what was taking place between us. It didn't feel like starting over it felt like picking up exactly where we left off.

"Mr. Thorn, can we get a statement please?" a news reporter stopped and asked him. I saw the gleam in his eye. This was what he was destined for. He was great in the media, he just had that aura that made you want to hear what he had to say. You knew it would be powerful. I waited as he did his best to look presentable. The Thorns had torn his shirt to shreds. His tattoo, bulging biceps and pecks were all on display.

"Vote for me." He spoke into the mic. Smiling up at him he wrapped his arm around my shoulders, kissed my forehead and we proceeded eager to get home to make up for lost time.

"Dame!" I heard her yelling. The sweet sound of her voice was something I looked forward to these days. It was normally her sweet nothings that woke up in the morning and put me to bed at night. Her voice carried so much love that I hung onto each word she said. It always sounded like she was singing to me. Her voice activated the butterflies and ignited the flames every day.

"Dame," she yelled again. Getting up I followed the voice to find her in the closet looking disheveled with clothes and dresses littering the floor. Tears where in her eyes and I wasn't sure what I had done.

"Rose, what's wrong?" I asked, kneeling in front of her.

"It's too much pressure, I'm not going." She huffed.

Today the announcement of the next senator was set to be declared. It was important for me to have her by my side. I had gone my whole career without her cheering me on like I knew she would. I wanted her there with me. I needed her there with me.

"Ain't no pressure love, what's wrong?"

"This is your big day, and I don't even have anything classy enough to wear to compliment you, and what are the people going to say?" she whined. This was a new side of Rose I wasn't used to. Rose was confident even when she wasn't. She didn't worry about what people thought of her and she damn sure didn't shrink around others.

"This is a new Rose, and I ain't fucking with it. Fuck them people, you comin' for me not for them. You don't have to prove yourself to them. Wear what you want as long as you come."

"No, I want a fancy-dress babe, I deserve a fancy dress. I want my hair done perfectly, I know that would make you happy." She continued to whine.

"I don't really want to hear that shit, you coming to support me is what would make me happy, knowing you are in the crowd instead of searching for you is what would make me happy. Its you not the clothes, not the hair, not the shoes, not those other people in attendance. You are what matters."

"Are you sure?"

"Positive, and plus, I got you a dress for tonight." I smiled as she wiped her tears. I took the initiative to get her dress because today would be special for more than one reason. I just needed her to dry her eyes and smile a little. Today would only be the beginning of a new day and life for us and the citizens of Avia.

"I'm sorry, I don't want to ruin your mood. I know you are happy, and I'm so proud of you. I'm just overreacting," she said standing up.

Us moving in together was intense. We argued for a week straight about closet space, food choices, cleaning and all the typical shit of sharing a living space but it was good for us. For once I was able to be human, I didn't have to be a yes man, I finally had a voice even if it was just with her. The circumstances of our situation showed me so much about myself. I had been a really selfish person, I had lived a life of not knowing what I liked and disliked. My life had developed into making time for what I was told to make time for , not what I wanted. Her lazy days made time for reflection, she had no idea how much I appreciated her for that. Eating pizza on the floor and reaching over her for more soda made me feel like a man on a quest to find out about me. I liked how easy it was for me to be happy. She never made me feel like I had to conform. I wanted to get back to that guy that laughed about silly shit, I wanted to be that guy that played my music way to loud because it made me feel good. I wanted what made me feel good, and that was her. Natural hair, natural face, natural spirit, and love that was enough to carry us both.

"I'm happy that you are here with me, ain't that enough?"

"Of course, but Thorn, our past haunts me in situations like this. I sincerely don't want to ruin what you have going on." She sighed.

"Don't try and figure out shit that ain't important. This is our course. The shit I said and did in the past was programmed. Those weren't my real feelings and I'm sorry I ever made you feel like you weren't good enough because the truth is I wasn't good enough for you. I was never taught to love the way you were. Everyday I'm getting a lesson on love. What me and you have is real."

"I feel the same way, it's just we are so different now, and I feel naïve for thinking that things won't change."

"Let your guard down, I won't fail you this time. Failing you would be failing myself." I urged.

"Let's go get this win." She smiled.

"Your dress and everything you need is in the bathroom."

I prayed my argument was convincing. I would say it over and over every day if I had to. I need her to understand that the wave we were riding would always be there and never be too much. We weren't asking too much from those around us. The request to allow us to love one another the way it should have been all those years ago was the only request we had. It required us to be confident or those naysayers would poke holes and we would sink. I needed her on board and confident in what we had and were trying to build. It would only be on us if we didn't make it. I wasn't prepared for that.

***

Stepping out of the limousine at town hall was unnerving. I didn't know what we were walking into. I didn't know if my argument was convincing enough to win the vote of the people. I practiced my speech over and over in my head but now it all seemed to flee. My heart was fluttering, and my smile was glued. I couldn't believe the verdict was finally in. In a matter of hours, I would know my fate.

"Relax, you got this. You are the only man for this job," she whispered smiling and waving to the cameras in her strapless black sequin dress. She wore it so well, so well that I could only imagine removing it later. If I didn't win that would be the highlight of my night, and the way it hugged her hips, I was alright with that.

"You look good Rose, you were worried for no reason." I said kissing her hand and pulling her seat out. The venue was nice, I wasn't impressed. I had been to so many events like this that it I felt myself slipping into my robotic state, ready to mingle and shake hands and pretend to be interested in Sam's seventh kid or Brenda's new casserole concoction.

"What do we do now?" she asked, looking around nervously.

"We wait and mingle. Want something to drink?"

"Yeah, if I'm required to mingle, Vodka tonic."

Leaving to get her drink I spotted a few people I wanted to avoid. My parents and the Wainwrights. Keeping my composure, I proceeded to the bar and ordered her drink. I didn't want to be under the influence while under construction. Things between me and my family had gotten odd and volatile. I wasn't arguing with Darlene today about any of my decisions.

Making it back to the table, she was gone. Looking around, I spotted her chatting with Colleen. Her warm smile let me know she was fine and going to do just fine. Still, I stared in admiration of her pulling it together for a cause I'm sure she didn't believe in. I couldn't blame her, politics were nasty, and everyone wasn't cut out for it. I prayed her strength activated when I needed her the most.

For the moment, she seemed to be doing just fine, with her natural hair. She attempted to straighten it for tonight, and I refused to allow her to do that thinking it was what I wanted. This night wasn't just about me, it was about us both. This was the first time we would be seen together as a couple. Making her change wasn't the course we were taking. I wanted her to be free to be who she was now that she was back. We still had a few things to work on but for the most part I loved her how she was, and I was sure others would also, and if not, fuck 'em.

"She looks amazing, Thorn." I heard from behind me. Looking over my shoulder, I came face to face with Erica and her blue-eyed date. Standing to my feet, we embraced. Although I was aware of her treachery, I still had love for Erica. We were both so much alike that the blame couldn't be put solely on her.

"Thank you, she's a natural, huh?" I asked. Rose was now making her rounds. She was carrying on like a true senator's wife, and I was proud, and as Erica mentioned, she looked beautiful doing it. The split on the side of the dress exposed her chocolate thighs and soft skin. I wasn't the only one in awe, and that let me know I made a good decision.

"Hey, listen, I wanted to apologize to you for everything," Erica said. I looked at her attempting see if this was a game.

"No apologies needed, if it wasn't for you, I'd still be without the love of my life. Thank you for bringing her back to me." I admitted kissing her cheek.

"That's good, because I'm finally able to love who I want to love. Meet Indigo."

"Indigo, nice to meet you, enjoy your night," I responded taking off to meet my woman and mingle. Walking up behind her, her perfume consumed my nostril prompting my inhale deeply. She was perfection, this was where I belonged all along. She was a classic beauty, and I felt the rush around her each time she was in the vicinity. My heart sang its own tune when she was near. Right now, our beats matched as I hugged her from behind. We were destined to be the next Michelle and Obama.

No More Wrong Turns

At first, I was fearful of being apart of this event. This wasn't my scene, but after careful consideration, there was no way I would be able to have him in the way I wanted without stepping out my comfort zone. It was more about proving to myself to him that I could do this. He said I didn't have to, but I knew damn well I did. I knew the first few years would be a test of our relationship and whether or not he had a point all those years.

"Rose, you doin' ok with all these uppity people?" Colleen asked. She was in attendance, and that allowed me to breathe a little easier than I was when we first walked in. The flashing lights, sea of white people, and nice cocktails spooked me, but I also reminded myself that he asked me to attend this.

"Yeah, bitch, I'm smiling and waving, smiling and waving." I laughed. I caught Damien staring out the corner of my eye. His black suit and white dress shirt looked amazing on him. I thought I appreciated him in sweatpants and a white tee but seeing him in the flesh in a nice suit with a nice haircut did something to me. I never took myself for the professional type, but he had a way of changing shit with no notice.

"Everything ok?" she asked.

"As to be expected, it's only been a month, it's still seemingly fresh." Raven's Pointe was a small town without a lot going on. It would be years before something as big as my scandal would divert the attention.

"It'll blow over, I promise." She alleged.

"Yeah in twenty years," I still felt the sting of last month's scandal. I wasn't in danger or fear of being arrested or hunted. It was the stares and silent conversations that worried and made me uncomfortable. I wasn't working allowing me time to focus getting my life back together. My apartment was ruined when the torch protesters came looking for me, they had also camped outside of my business with the pitch forks. I wanted a moment of peace.

"Tru, I miss you at work, please come save me from myself." She begged. I missed it also, but after graduation, I hit the ground running climbing my way to success. I hadn't enjoyed being a woman in her late twenties. I hadn't travelled, I hadn't enjoyed the bed enough, I hadn't enjoyed the art of figuring me out. I needed a moment to find myself. Work would get in the way, not to mention I wondered if the playing field was even fair anymore. Now that people questioned me having powers. Shit was weird, and I didn't want to stress myself, so I was taking time. Taking time to spend it with Damien, with my momma and with myself.

"I can't right now, boo, I miss it too, but I'm enjoying my situation right now." I winked. Me and Damien had been fucking like rabbits, eating junk food, catching up on movies. It felt like college all over again. It felt like we were best friends again just adding benefits. I was happy and full of joy. Happy had the opportunity to fade, but I had joy in my heart that would remain as long as I took care of it.

"Gross." She laughed.

"How is Ryan? And what about Carlos" I asked. Unsure why after all the trouble he caused me over the years. From these damn uncontrollable powers, to testing my patience and ultimately attempting to have put under the jail. Still, I felt sorry for him. I was confident that the whole crew wasn't that different. We were all living up to someone else's standards, and that type of pressure could crack and bust even the strongest pipes. I happened to be a casualty again of doing what others wanted.

"Ryan is Ryan, he's in the islands apparently doing marine biology." She shrugged. "And me and Carlos are doing great. I didn't know he was such a gentleman. He's someone around here."

Melting, I felt his arms around my waist and smelled our body scents melting. It didn't get any better than this. Lately, I've heard nothing but how much Thorn loved me and how beautiful and perfect I was. We hadn't been here before, and it was refreshing to hear his feelings for me instead of attempting to read between the lines.

"Hey you, enjoying yourself?" I asked.

"Not really, but it's a part of it. How about you?"

"I anticipated a little bit of discomfort, but it's going good, you remember Colleen, right?" I asked joking. I needed them to bury the hatchet and quickly. We were moving on, and she needed to also.

"Yeah, hey, Colleen."

"Oh, Damien, stop the shit. You fuck up this time, I'll go down in history for assassinating the senator. Rose, I'll call you tomorrow, let's do lunch."

Hugging her goodbye, I grabbed Damien's hand just as the announcer reached the podium. It was time, and his grip was so tight, I thought he would break my hand. His nervous state was charming. He was always so calm and collected, but right now, the chewing on the inside of his lip, moving from foot to foot and checking his suit was telling a different story.

"You need to relax, Senator Thorn," I whispered in his ear. His grip loosened and turned to look into my eyes. Things were shaping up perfectly for us. Things were in sync finally, and I was feeling a little bashful that I had exactly what I was looking for after all this time.

"Ladies and gentlemen, it's been a tight race, and there can only be one senator. Damien and Skylar, you've done an exceptional job, and I know that whoever wins will be a great asset to Avia."

My mind drifted to what this would mean if he won. It was too late to get scared now about dating a senator. It was too late to run and hide. His grip tightened, and his smile widened as I tuned back into the dinner party. Everyone from the town was cheering and waiting for the results. I wasn't sure what I was waiting on. I may have been waiting on a sign that hadn't come just yet. I was starting to sweat and fidget.

"Rose, what's wrong?" he asked. I couldn't make a sound. All I could do was stare at him and calculate all the ways I would fuck up his life. I didn't want to do that. I couldn't do that. He said he didn't care, but who wanted to be on the front of magazines with a wife that had little class and status?

Stepping back, I looked around me at everyone in attendance; no one was focused on me. No one was whispering and pointing. No one was attempting to jade me and make me feel less than, and I had Thorn in front of me, with me. I was tripping and needed to snap out of it quickly.

"I'm fine, I was just having a moment," I replied kissing his soft lips.

"I have a question for you really quick before it gets crazy in here," he said kneeling in front of me. "I know it's kinda fast, and I said for you to think about it, but I really need to know like today. No matter what's happened between me and you, you've always stayed with me and had a major role in my success. One day, you told me to make sure it was worth it, well it was. I needed this last test to reveal to me whether this was what I wanted. I do want it, but I want you with me. You will always be the rose to my thorn, but I need it to be official. Will you be Mrs. Thorn? Will you match my super powers? Will you be the reason I live and breathe? Will you accept that I'm a man with many flaws and that made a mistake turning my back on you and thinking I could do it without you?" he asked teary eyed.

"Yes, but I need to confess that I am willing to be all that you need and desire, but I won't be changed. I still want to be me, and I need to know that that's what you want forever, not because we are in the moment and because things are good right now."

"There's no doubt in my mind that I want to meet you at the altar. I'm under construction myself, and I would never ever ask that of you again. Marry me, Tru!"

"Let's do it, Damien." I cried.

"Your new senator is Damien Thorn, Congratulations, this young man came out swinging and has won over Avia and for good reason. Let's give him a round of applause," the announcer said as I was spun in midair.

"We won," he cheered. Watching him saunter with all his swag to the podium caused the widest smile to adorn my face. He did it, he won despite all the chips stacked against him.

"Wow, yall, I can't believe we did it. Skylar, it was a tight race, and you did a great job. Please give him a round of applause as well." He paused and winked at me. I winked back uber proud of the win and all the success that came with him, both personal and career wise. "Tonight is important and dope for several reasons. Winning is just a part of it, but winning over the love of my life and her accepting my hand in marriage is by far the highlight of my night. Rose, thank you for making me the happiest man alive, and to Raven's Pointe, thank you for all your votes and trusting me to turn things around. Enjoy your night."

The spotlight was on me as he made his way to me from the podium. The crowd was cheering, and the confetti and balloons were falling around us. This was a beautiful moment. I smiled and waited for him to reach me, and when he did, I felt like I was in a wonderland as he kissed me so passionately and spun me around again.

"We did it, baby." He breathed into my mouth.

"You deserve it, my love." I breathed back as if no one was in the room with us. People were clapping and congratulating us, but all I could see was him. All I could think about was loving him forever in any kind of way I could.

We did it despite all the chips stacked against us. Finally, the Thorn to my Rose was back like he had never left. We were complete as it was supposed to be. We beat the odds.

The End

A letter to my readers

Thank you all for the support. I hope you have enjoyed this novel as much I enjoyed writing it. This is a different story for me, but I hope you enjoy it the same. It's my prayer that this title goes down as one of your favorites. I worked really hard on creating something that would set me apart from the crowd.

If you are reading this that means you've reached the end, so again Thank you and please leave me a review. I always look forward to your feedback, good, bad, or indifferent. A year ago no one would be able to tell me that I would have 8 books published. I'm grateful and blessed for the opportunity.

I am always looking for new readers and supporters. Because without you this dream wouldn't be real.

Wanna connect with me and my readers? Join my reading group for laughs, prizes, sneak peeks all of the good stuff!!

https://www.facebook.com/groups/499040183779085/

IG:

https://www.instagram.com/author_cmonet/

Author Page:

https://www.facebook.com/authorc.money/

Website:

www.unfilteredandundefined.com